I0713243

BATTLE CRIES OF THE
AMERICAN
FLAGS

MICKEY DENNIS

I pledge allegiance to the Flag of the United States of America, and to the Republic for which it stands, one nation, under God, indivisible, with liberty and justice for all.

Zeta Publishing, Inc
P.O. Box 953
Silver Springs, FL 34489
www.zetapublishing.com

The views expressed in this work are solely those of the author and do not necessarily reflect the views of the publisher, and the publisher hereby disclaims any responsibility for them.

Ordering Information:
Quantity sales. Special discounts are available on quantity purchases by corporations, associations, and others. For details, contact the publisher at the address above.
Orders by U.S. trade bookstores and wholesalers. Please contact Zeta Publishing: Tel: (352) 694-2553; Fax: (352) 694-1791 or visit www.zetapublishing.com

First published by Xlibris Corp

Rev. Date: August 2019

ISBN: 978-1-950340-14-9 (sc)
ISBN: 978-1-950340-15-6 (e)

Library of Congress: 2019909980
Printed in the United States of America

INTRODUCTION

We do honor to the stars and stripes as the emblem of our country, we identify the flag with almost everything we hold dear on earth. It represents our peace and security, our civil and political liberty, freedom of religious worship, our family our friend, our home. We see it in the multitude of blessing, when we look at our flag and behold the multitude of our rights, we must never forget that it is equally a symbol of our duties. Every glory that we associate with it is the result of duty that has already been done. This land the people and the flag, this nation a continent every race, the flag a symbol of what humanity may aspire to when we are all at peace, each generation must be dedicated and consecrated anew, too defend with life it self, need be, but, above all, in friendliness, in hope, in courage, to live for.

DEDICATION

I dedicate this book to all military veterans who have served and are now serving the United States in times of war and peace.

MICKEY'S WORDS OF WISDOM

I urge you to accept the greatest test of all, living when there seems nothing to live for; I promise you, if you survive the darkest minutes, then you will live to see better days. Utter despair is endurable with help reach our during that despair and you will live to help others live.

I pledge allegiance to the flag.

I can vividly recall, as a child, viewing a parade in my hometown. The crowd stood by the curb anxiously waiting as the sound of music came ever closer. Finally, I felt my heart jump, and my body chill. Some of the people saluted while others placed a hand on their heart. It was the American Flag! To this day, whether it's a parade, a concert, or a ballgame, I thrill to the sight of our flag, and I have a feeling that you feel the same way that I do. I see more than stars and stripes.

Please, let me share with you why I am so thrilled, so in love and enthusiastic about this American icon. Come; take a trip with me, back into history.

Close your eyes, relax, and set your mind at ease. Now open your eyes, where are we?

What happened? How in the world did we get here? That is not important at the moment, what is important, is the *birth* of the American Flag.

We are now at the home of Sam and Rebecca Griscom. They are the parents of Elizabeth Griscom. Who is she, you ask? My friend, she is the mother, who will give birth to an American symbol, freedom, plenty, pride, that patriotic fervor that will stand the test of time that will symbolize hope for an entire race. What we see and witness here, are the creation of a symbol that will bring forth a new nation. Wow! All that? Yes. What does Elizabeth, or any of these people have to do with the creation of this great nation? Look at these people, their poor, uneducated, and simple in life. Just see how they dress, what kind of get-up is this? Yes, they are simple, but not in their heart, poor in money sure, but no in spirit. Tell me, why I should concern myself over a piece of cloth.

Today's date, 1752, state, Philadelphia, Pennsylvania, January 1 at the home of Elizabeth Griscom's parents home. There are many questions about the American flags that most people don't know, and don't understand, or don't care.

Before we begin, we need to go back to the beginning. The English began to settle colonies in North America 100 years after Spain did. To offset the cost of starting a colony, joint stock companies were formed. Many of the people gave money to share the costs. As part owners in this new colony, they had to share the profits and risk as well. In 1607, three English ships landed in what is today called Virginia. These settlers named the colony Jamestown, to honor King James of England. Many of these people died from hunger and a number of diseases that first year that they were there.

"These people could use our help! We must do something! No we cannot get involved, remember this is not our time. This is too much for me? Can we leave this place? WAIT! Things will get better, trust me."

When things seemed hopeless, a man named John Smith, the leader of the colony, made friends with the Native Americans. He obtained enough food to help the colonists live through their first winter. In 1612, some settler decided to grow what they had seen the Native Americans grow. They grew tobacco, and it grew well in the swampy soil. By1619, tobacco became Jamestown's biggest cash crop.

"See, now this is better; this John Smith is some guy!"

Now these growers offered to pay for workers to come from England to Jamestown, these people were known as indentured servants. In 1619, the first African arrived in Jamestown.

"Why would they bring these people there? Well they need someone to pick the tobacco. Ok I see. No you don't. Oh my gosh! Are these people what I think they are? YES! Slaves!

Slaves? Why do they need these people? Cheap labor that is why. Most farmers found it better to have slaves than indentured servants. Slaves, I don't think that is good! You are right, it is not."

In the 1600's, people in England were being punished for their religious beliefs, so many did not agree with the beliefs of the Church of England. This group was the pilgrims, and around 1620, these pilgrims, 101 of them boarded the ship, Mayflower. The people were fed up with the king! They wanted to be free; they wanted to follow their own religious beliefs. Two months later, they landed in the area we know today as Massachusetts. Before leaving the ship, the leaders of the pilgrims wrote an agreement saying this colony will be fair and equal.

Everyone on board agreed to this law. *"What about the slaves? How do they fit into all this? A good question!"* The pilgrim colony was named Plymouth. In the fall of 1621, the pilgrims held a three-day harvest festival, which was later to be known as Thanksgiving. *"Look at all this food! Can we eat? I am hungry? The food did look good, I must say."*

Self-government had just been born in America. How, by the Mayflower contract. A vote was taken to decide if the laws of the Mayflower contract should be followed. The New England colonies grew, and each citizen took part in every issue that affected their towns. In 1628, another group of settlers came to New England. Like the pilgrims, they wanted to be free to follow their religious beliefs. These people were called Puritans, because they wanted to make the Church of England more "pure". By 1630, the Puritans had settled a large colony that they called the Massachusetts Bay Colony. These Puritans began to build settlements near their most important town, Boston. These Puritans came here to the Americas for religious freedom, but the leaders did not want the others to have a choice. The other had no choice and if anyone who did not follow church laws was punished. So many of the settlers began to move, yet again to other areas of New England. There were 13 English colonies established along the Atlantic coast between 1607 and 1733. The Massachusetts Bay Colony was the first New England Colony. At that time, this colony included all the land in present day Massachusetts and part of present day Maine. After Massachusetts was settled, many people who were unhappy with the Puritan life, moved to other areas and there were some that were forced to move.

So in 1635, a minister, who was named Roger Williams, was ordered to move. The reason that he was forced to move was because he believed the Church had to much power, the two should be separate, and all the people should be free to practice their own beliefs. So he and those who felt as he did built their own settlement and called it Providence. A colony in what we call Rhode Island. Here all people were free to follow their religious beliefs. There was also another person who was also a puritan, and she as well, did not agree with all the Puritan ministers. This woman, Anne Hutchinson, and those who followed her were also unhappy with the beliefs of the Puritans, so eventually, Hutchinson was put on trial. She was found guilty.

She had to go, so she and her family left the colony in 1638, and with a group of followers, she helped to settle in a new colony in Rhode Island.

In 1839 settlers in Connecticut wrote a document called the Fundamental Order of Connecticut. Simply put, the people would live by its rules; the Fundamental Orders became the first written system of government in North America. In 1623, King James the first of England sent merchants and others to explore this coast of present-day New Hampshire. Soon other people came to these communities from Massachusetts. They had had enough of the Puritan Church. New Hampshire became a colony in 1741. During the 1600' s people from the Netherlands claimed much of the land between Virginia and New Hampshire. These people were called Dutch. In 1609, Henry Hudson and explorers were paid by these Dutch people to sail upriver, which were later named for him. Both sides of the river were claimed. In 1626, the land was named New Netherlands. The largest town in that colony was settled on an island where the Manhattan group of Native Americans lived. The new town was called New Amsterdam. This land claimed by the Netherlands people did not stay under Dutch control very long. In 1664, English forces took control of New Amsterdam and the rest of the colony. The land was broken into smaller colonies, such as New York, and New Jersey, and the large town at the mouth of the Hudson was renamed New York City. Like New Jersey, it too attracted European Nations.

In 1681, William Penn, a Quaker, was allowed to settle a colony called Pennsylvania. The Quakers believed that all people should be treated fairly, even the slaves. Now the quakes signed a peace treaty with the Native Americans. Pennsylvania became a colony known for its freedom.

Settlers from Sweden came too what is now known as Delaware. In 1638, these Swedish built a settlement and named it Fort Christiana, and they built others as well. Delaware became a colony in 1704.

The first colony of Virginia began with the Jamestown settlement in 1607. Jamestown began to attract settlers from the New England, and middle colonies, and more settlers came from England. In England, people were punished for their religious beliefs, sometimes were even killed for them. In 1632, a man named Lord Baltimore, who was rich and very religious, was given a charter. He settled the colony of Maryland. In 1649, Lord Baltimore made sure that the Toleration Act was passed in Maryland. This act guaranteed freedom of religion to all.

In 1663, King Charles of England gave eight rich English lords the right to settle land south of Virginia and that land was called the Carolinas after the English King. Settlers in Carolina had their religious freedom. Many had heard about this and the very rich soil as well. So many people came to Carolina and it was then broken into two parts, North and South Carolina. Of all places, Georgia, was the last colony. Georgia was settled to give homes to debtors, which were known as people who would not pay their bills. A man named James Oglethorpe, who felt is was unfair to put debtors in jail. He went to the king to ask for a new start, and allow these people to settle in America. In 1733, Georgia, named after King George II, became the 13th English colony.

"Thirteen colonies, Georgia, South Carolina, North Carolina, Maryland, Virginia, Pennsylvania, New York, Delaware, New Jersey, Connecticut, Rhode Island, Maine and New Hampshire. So there we have it. Man, we covered a lot of territory. Yes we did. I am ready for home, how about you? Not yet. We have much, much more to cover. What is next you ask?

What about a trip to Africa? Why Africa? Because, my friend, it is the darkest period in the history of mankind. Well, what happened?"

Along the coast, and the southern colonies used large plantations to farm and when word got out that cheap labor was bountiful and the supply was easy. The reason was slaves. By the 1700's enslaved Africans were doing all the work on these plantations of the south. These people were brought to this country in large ships, they were treated very cruelly from the moment they boarded the ships till almost the day that they died. These people were crammed in the below deck, these voyages formed three points of a great triangle on the Atlantic Ocean. The triangular route connected to the states to West Africa and to the West Indies. To make this work, the first part of the route, ships would carry goods from the colonies to West Africa.

There, the goods were traded for enslaved Africans. On the second part of the route, ships leaving West Africa carried enslaved Africans to sell to the West Indies. This part of the trip was called the Middle Passage.

Colonial settlements grew into cities and towns. The colonists developed new ways of doing things. They began to think of themselves as separate from England. These colonies were divided into three regions. These were the New England, Middle and Southern colonies. Each region had its own climate, economy, and way of life. There were many changes in the colonies from 1630 to 1760, some settlements became towns, and some towns along the Atlantic Coast became cities. By the middle of the 1700's many colonists no longer felt like a part of Great Britain. There were new ideas about religion, politics and economics.

As more British settlers came to North America, they traveled farther west. By the middle of the 1700's they had pushed over the Appalachian Mountains into the Ohio River Valley.

However, France had already explored that region. Now there were two enemies from Europe, Great Britain and France, who fought in those less settled areas of North America. When the French explorers landed, they were not looking for gold; they were looking for fur. After building a settlement In Quebec, Canada, the French fur traders traveled in canoes across the Great Lakes and down the Ohio River to the Mississippi River. These fur traders got along well with many of the Native Americans. They traded fairly for furs and they treated the natives as equals.

During the 1750's, fur traders from Great Britain began to cross the Appalachian Mountains. Soon Great Britain claimed the land that the French had named New France. Both France and Britain wanted to control the valley. That led, of course, to war. In 1754, Great Britain and France went to war. Now the natives felt it was better to help the French. This war became known as the French and Indian War.

It seemed as first that France was winning the war. In one battle, the French forces beat the colonial troops led by a young officer named George Washington. In another battle, French and Native American forces attacked and killed about 900 British soldiers. Soon Great Britain began sending more troops and supplies to the colonies. Then in 1760, British troops and colonists attacked the large French post in Quebec. By 1763, the fighting had ended. France's power in North America was over. The British claimed the Ohio River Valley. France had to leave or surrender. Great Britain also took control of Canada. After the French and Indian war, King George III passed a law saying that colonists could not settle in the Ohio River Valley. This law was called the Proclamation Of 1763. Now this law angered the colonists and some of the other laws that the king made, had them even angrier. This Proclamation of 1763 was only the beginning of new laws. Over the next several years, British rulers passed four more acts of law. These included the Sugar Act, the Stamp Act, and Quartering Act and the money that was collected in taxes went back to Great Britain. The colonists wanted to use the money to improve the quality of life for themselves. The colonists protested, or spoke and acted against the new British laws. Some colonists refused to buy British goods, while others refused to pay the taxes. Protest groups called the Sons of Liberty were formed Colonial leaders, such as Patrick Henry and Samuel

Adams, spoke out against the taxes. "No taxation without representation!" Which later became a famous saying.

Bad feelings soon became strong between the colonists and British soldiers. On March 5, 1770, a crowd of colonists in Boston began to yell insults at a group of British soldiers.

Someone began to throw snowballs and suddenly a British soldier was hit with a rock. Shots rang out. That day, five colonial men died in what became known as the Boston Massacre.

After this fight, the British finally understood how angry the colonists were. The British decided to repeal or end, most of the towns' head acts. However, Kind George III said that the tax idea had to remain. It would remind colonists that they were still under British control. The colonists' anger continued to grow, and finally they took matters into their own hands. On December 1773, some colonists dressed as Native Americans, boarded British ships in the Boston Harbor. This ship was loaded with tea. So the colonists threw all that tea overboard.

Led by Samuel Adams, this became known as the Boston Tea Party. In 1774, colonial leaders met in Philadelphia, Pennsylvania. George Washington, Samuel Adams, and Patrick Henry were among the leaders that were present. This was the first meeting of the Continental Congress. Representatives came from every colony, except Georgia, came to that historical meeting. Those who met sent a declaration of American Rights to the king. This declaration listed all the unfair treatment that the colonists felt that they had received. However, this declaration did not change the actions of the British Government. So the colonists had to rethink their idea. This problem between Great Britain and the colonies just got worse.

Patrick Henry's speech angered the British when he cried out; "Give me liberty or give me death!" Those words rang throughout the colonies, and he was not the only one ready to die. In Massachusetts, groups of men called Minutemen were formed in most towns. From age 16 to 60, they could be ready to fight at a minute's notice.

On the morning of April 19, 1775, the British arrived at Lexington Green. Seventy men were waiting to stop this large British force. American Captain John Parker gave the orders. "Stand your ground. Don't fire unless fired upon, but if they want war, let it begin here!"

No one knows who fired the first shot, but within a few minutes, eight colonists lay dead. The Minutemen scattered in defeat. General Gage's troops marched on to the Concord. However, there were not beaten. As the British reached the North Bridge in Concord, there were met by a larger force of Minutemen. More than 450 farmers, shopkeepers and others had rifles ready.

They charged across the North Bridge, forcing the British to turn back to Boston. Along the road, more Minutemen joined in the fight. About a month after the Battles of Lexington and Concord, the leaders met again in Philadelphia. This meeting was called the Second Continental Congress. War had not yet been declared between Great Britain and the colonies. The leaders did not want to go to war. However, the colonials made every effort to find a peaceful solution to their problems. The solution that was finally offered was called the Olive Branch Petition. At the same time colonial leaders decided to prepare for war. They chose George Washington, a Virginia planter, as their military leader. While this second Continental Congress was going on in Philadelphia, more fighting was breaking out in Boston. After a bloody battle, Britain forces took Bunker Hill on June 17, 1775. The losses shocked King George III. He ordered the British Navy to keep all supply ships from reaching the colonies.

He also hired German soldiers called Hessians to help control the colonists.

King George sent 30,000 more troops to the colonies. In June 1776, the second Continental Congress gave a young colonist from Virginia an important job. His name was Thomas Jefferson. He was asked to write a declaration explaining why the colonies should be free from British rule. At that time, equality and liberty were thought by some to be the rights of white men only. The colonists, who signed this declaration, basically told Great Britain and the world, "That these united colonies are, and of right ought to be free and independent states." The 13 colonies had declared their independence at last.

Those colonists who remained loyal to Great Britain were also known as Loyalists and those who wanted their independence were called patriots, and there were some who did not care who won the war, they were declared neutral. The colonists were fighting against one of the toughest and best trained armies in the world. George Washington knew that his best chance of defeating the stronger British forces was with surprise attack. October 25, 1777, a force of American volunteers met a large British force in Saratoga, New York. The battle was fought off and on for several weeks. Finally, British forces surrendered to the Americas. This battle was called The Turning Point of the war, because it sent an important message to other countries. France, who was one of Great Britain's enemies, started to believe that American would win the war against Great Britain. The French began to send supplies to the Americans. At Saratoga, General Benedict Arnold led American troops, but Arnold soon became a traitor to the Americans. Arnold joined up with the British forces and gave away American military secrets, those were early battles of the war.

The war for Independence, which was also called the Revolutionary War, was a hard fought war. It ended in victory for all of America. June 14, 1777, America adopted their first flag.

The Grand Union Flag, which was the first US flag adapted in 1776 and was used during the American Revolutionary War by George Washington at the time of the signing of the Declaration of Independence on July 4, 1776. The United States had no official national flag. Although it has never had an official status, it was used to inspire a new nation, a new era of brotherhood, an independence of freedom and liberty and the pursuit of happiness.

The first US flag had a circle of stars representing the first thirteen colonies of the United States of America. *"So, we have our first flag! Yes, we do!"* Many will come to understand the flag to represent freedoms for all and the rights guaranteed in the constitution and it's Bill of Rights and most of all, it is a symbol of individual and personal liberty as set forth in the Declaration of Independence.

The Flag Resolution of 1777

On June 4, 1777, the Marine committee of the second continental Congress passed the flag resolution which stated: "Resolved, that the flag of the United States be thirteen stripes, alternate red and white, and that the Union be thirteen stars, white in a blue field, representing a new constellation. The Continental Army at the Middlebrook Encampment first raised this flag June 1777. In 1795, the number of stars and stripes was increased from 13 to 15 to reflect the entry of Vermont and Kentucky as states of the Union. For a time, the flag was not changed when subsequent states were admitted, probably because it was thought that this would cause too much clutter. It was the 15 stars and 15 stripes flag that inspired Francis Scott Key to write the **Star Spangled Banner,** which is now the National Anthem. In June 1776, Thomas Pains published a pamphlet called *Common Sense.* In it he said that colonists should rule themselves by setting up their own government. He said kings only brought misery to their people and should be overthrown. The new congress read Paine's pamphlet, and many of the members agreed with his ideas. In June 1776, the Second Continental Congress gave a young colonist from Virginia an important job. That was Thomas Jefferson. He was asked to write a declaration explaining why the colonies should be free from British rule. In the declaration, Jefferson tried to speak for all the colonists. He said that colonists believed in equality. He said that colonists believed that they had the right to life, liberty and the pursuit of happiness, but at that time, equality and liberty were thought by some to be the rights of white men only. Finally, on July 4, 1776, all the members of the Second Continental Congress signed the Declaration of Independence. The colonists who signed it told Great Britain and the world, "that these United Colonies are, and of right ought to be free and independent states." The 13 colonies had declared their independence. The war for independence, which is also called the Revolutionary War, it was a hard fought war. It ended in victory for the Americans.

Summer of 1776: Battle of New York

George Washington was badly out numbered, but they were defeating the powerful British fleet.

December 25, 1776: Battle of Trenton

On Christmas Eve, the American troops crossed the Delaware River in the dark of the night.

They marched to Trenton and captured more than 900 Hessians. Only four Americans were wounded. Trenton was the first American victory, since independence had been declared. It raised the hopes of the Patriots everywhere.

October 17, 1777: Battle of Saratoga

This battle was called the Turning Point of the war because it sent an important message to other countries.

Winter 1778: Valley Forge

A few months after the victory at Saratoga, American forces hit their lowest point at Valley Forge, Pennsylvania. While the British troops were safe and warm in nearby Philadelphia, thousands of Americans froze to death in the cold. After the American victory at

Saratoga, Benjamin Franklin went to France to get help for the United States. He worked with the French leader to put together a treaty between the United States and France. The French were then ready to join the American fight for independence. The French nobleman, Marquis Lafayette had come to Virginia to join the Americans a year earlier. When French troops arrived, he led them against the British forces in the south. Once France decided to help the American side, it opened the way for other countries to join in the war. Spain and Holland lent money to help the Americans. The German Military leader Baron Von Steuben served as a leader for American Troops. So did military leaders from Poland, including Count Pulaski and Thaddeus Kosciusko.

Fall of 1781: Battle of Yorktown

British General Lord Cornwallis marched through the south. Finally he was trapped on a piece of land near Yorktown, Virginia, which was surrounded on three sides by water. The French navy blocked the British ships from rescuing Cornwallis's troops. The British were trapped. On October 19, 1781, Cornwallis surrendered. The United Sates of American was now a free country. Next the declaration described the colonists' main ideas about government.

Jefferson wrote, *"We hold these truths to be self-evident, that all men are created equal, that they are endowed by their creator with certain unalienable rights, that among these are life, liberty and the pursuit of happiness."* The war for independence ended, the 13 colonies won their freedom from Great Britain. However, there was still a great deal of work to do. The colonies had to create a new government and this would take time.

In 1776 the Bennington Military Flag was flown during the battle of the American Revolutionary War. That took place on August 16, 1777, in Wolloomsac, New York. Ten miles away from

Bennington, Vermont, an American force of2,000 New Hampshire and the Massachusetts militiamen, let by General John Stark with aid from Colonel Seth Warner, along with elements of Vermont's green mountain boys, defeated a combined force of1,250 dismounted Brunswick Dragoons, Canadians, Loyalists and Native Americans led by Lt. Colonel Fredrick Baum, that British General John Burgoyne was attempting to push through the Northern Hudson River Valley. After the recent British victories at Hubbardston, Fort Ticonderoga and St. Clair, Burgoyne's plan was to defeat the American Forces and then continue south to Albany and onto the Hudson River Valley. Dividing the American colonies in half. This was part of a grand plan to divide the rebellious New England colonies from the more loyal remaining colonies via a three-way pincer movement. However, the western pincer was repulsed and the southern pincer, which was to progress up the Hudson Valley from New York City, never started since General Howe decided to attack Philadelphia instead of helping Burgoyne. General Brum found himself near Bennington on a foraging mission to supply Burgoyne's large number of horses and to supply his soldiers with food.

On August 13, 1777, en route to Bennington, Baum learned of the arrival in the area of 1,500 New Hampshire militiamen under command of General John Stark, who, against, General Washington's wishes, had decided to fortify the town of Bennington. Baum ordered his forces to stop at Wolloomsac River, about four miles west of Bennington. After sending a request for reinforcements to Fort Miller, Baum took advantage of the terrain and deployed his forces on the high ground. In the rain, Baum's men constructed a small redoubt at the crest of the hill and hoped that the weather would prevent the Americans from attacking before reinforcements arrived.

Deployed a few miles away, Stark decided to reconnoiter Baum's positions and wait until the weather cleared. On the afternoon of August 16, 1777, the weather cleared, and Stark ordered his men ready to attack. Stark is reputed to have rallied his troops by saying, *"There are your enemies, the Red Coats and the Tories. They are ours, or this night Molly Stark sleeps a widow."* Upon hearing that the militia had melted away into the woods, Baum assumed that the Americans were retreating or redeploying. However, Stark had recognized that Baum's forces were spread thin and decided immediately to envelop them from two sides while simultaneously charging Baum's central redoubt head-on. The loyalists and Native Americans fled. This left Baum and his Brunswick dragoons trapped alone on the high ground. The Germans fought valiantly even after running low on powder. The dragoons lead a saber charge and tried to break through the enveloping forces. However, after this final charge failed and Baum was mortally wounded, the Germans surrendered. Shortly after this battle ended, while the New Hampshire militia were disarming the German troops, Baum's reinforcements arrived. The German reinforcements, under the command of Lt. Col. Heinrich Von Breymann, saw the Americans in disarray and pressed their attack immediately. After hastily regrouping, Stark's forces tried to hold their ground against the German onslaught before their lines collapsed, a group, Warner, had been defeated at the battle of Hub Barton by British reinforcements and were eager to exact their revenge on the enemy. Together, the New Hampshire and Vermont militia repulsed and finally stopped Breymann's force. Total German and British losses at Bennington were recorded at 207 dead and 700 captured; American losses included 40 Americans dean and 30 wounded. Stark's decision to intercept and destroy the raiding party before they could reach Bennington was a crucial factor in Burgoyne's eventual surrender, because it deprived his army of supplies. The American victory at Bennington also galvanized the rebels and was a catalyst for French involvement in the war.

The Flag Attributed to Betsy Ross

This flag is an early design of American Flag popularly attributed to Betsy Ross, using the common motifs of alternating red and white striped field with white stars in a blue canton. The flag was designed during the American Revolution and features 13 stars to represent the original 13 colonies. The distinctive features of the Ross flag are the arrangement the 5 pointed stars in a circle. The original Betsy Ross flag was made in 1776, when a small committee including George Washington and George Ross, a relative, visited Betsy and discussed the need for a new American flag. Betsy's contribution to the design was a five-pointed star instead of a six-pointed star, as Francis Hopkinson used, and she accepted the job to sew the flag. This flag was also used by 1777; Alfred B Street described it at the surrender of General Burgoyne and understood the circle of the stars to represent equality among the American states. The Second Continental Congress passes the Flag Resolution, establishing the first congressional standard for the official United States flag. The shape and arrangement of the stars is not mentioned, but the legal description gives the Ross flag true legitimacy. Resolved that the flag of the United States be thirteen stars, white in a blue field representing a new constellation.

The seal of the US Veterans administration uses the Betsy Ross flag to represent service to all veterans from the American Revolution to the present day. The Betsy Ross flag continues to be one of the most popular symbols of the American Revolution. In 1795, the numbers of the stars and stripes was increased from 13 to 15 to reflect the entry of Vermont and Kentucky as states of the Union. For a time, this flag was not changed when subsequent states were admitted. It was the 15 star, 15 striped flag that, as we know inspired our National Anthem.

On April 14, 1818, there was a plan that Congress, at the suggestion of US Navel Captain Samuel C. Reid, in which the flag should be changed to have 20 stars, with a new star to be added when each new state was admitted, but in the number of stripes would remain at 13 to honor the original colonies.

Francis Hopkinson of New Jersey, a signer of the Declaration of Independence, designed one of the most popular flags of the original 13 states, 1777 flag while he was the chairman of the continental navy board middle department, sometime between his appointment to that position in November 1776 and the time that the Flag Resolution was adapted in June 1777.

The flag of 1861 used during the Civil War, had 34 stars and 13 stripes. This flag is considered to be the most important flag flown in the history of the United States.

The American Civil War (1861-1865), also known as the War Between the States and a few other names, was a war in the United States. The war, the deadliest in American history, caused 620,000 soldiers deaths and an undetermined number of civilian casualties, ended slavery in the United States, restored the Union, and strengthened the role of the Federal Government. The social, political, economic and racial issues of the war dishevel snapped the reconstruction era that lasted to 1877, and continued into the 20th century.

Five days after the Civil War ended, President Lincoln went to a play at Ford Theater in Washington D.C. While he was at the play, he was assassinated, or murdered by John Wilkes Booth, who was a confederate supporter. Lincoln died the next day, on April 15, 1865 of a gunshot wound to the head. After the Civil War, the United States had many problems, but President Lincoln had approved the Thirteenth Amendment to the Constitution, finally outlawing slavery.

The New Government Begins The First President

On April 6, 1789, George Washington was elected the first president of the United States. John Adams, who finished second in the votes, became the first Vice-president. George served for two four-year terms as President, and during that time the country became stronger. George Washington accomplished the following: he kept the United States out of war, he raised enough money to pay off the country's war debt, he established a national bank, and finally he set up a money system. In 1796, Washington decided to step down as president, so in 1796, John Adams was elected the second president of the U.S. Adams became unpopular in 1880, thus losing the election to Thomas Jefferson.

The Louisiana Purchase

When Thomas Jefferson became president, he and the Congress quickly approved the sale and the Louisiana Purchase became a part of the United States on December 20, 1803. In 1804, President Jefferson sent Captain Meriwether Lewis and Lt. William Clark on an expedition.

Lewis and Clark had some help along the way; a Native American woman named Sacagawea became their guide. She traveled with them from what is now North Dakota, through Oregon. In November 1805, Lewis and Clark reached the Pacific Ocean. By September 1806, they were back in St. Louis. Later they met with the president. They had made many maps and gathered all types of plants, and animal samples, and for years settlers studied that information when they traveled to the Pacific Coast.

The War of 1812

Before the United States declared war, Great Britain had agreed to stop impressing Americans. The agreement arrived too late. The war of 1812 between Great Britain and the United States had begun. Both the U.S. and Great Britain had problems while fighting the war of 1812. The war lasted only two and half years. There was no winner and no loser. In 1814, the Treaty of Ghent was signed, ending the War of 1812.

The Monroe Doctrine

In 1816, James Monroe was elected President. During this time, European Nations controlled many colonies in the Americas. By 1823, almost all the colonies belonging to Spain had won their freedom. President Monroe wanted European counties out of America. In 1823, President Monroe gave a speech. "I promise to protect the freedom of countries on the American Continent". He warned Europe not to start any new colonies, or try to get back any old ones or enlarge any that are still here. He also promised, in return, which the United States would stay out of European problems. This speech became known as the Momoe Doctrine. In 1824, John Quincy Adams was elected the sixth president of the U.S. Four years later, in 1812, Andrew Jackson, a hero of the war of 1812, was elected President. His way of governing, or running the country was different from past presidents. Jackson believed in helping the common man.

Jackson's Native American Policies

Under pressure from Jackson, Congress passed the Indian Removal Act in 1830. All Indians east of the Mississippi River had to give up their land. They were also told that they would be given new land west of the Mississippi River. Some Native Americans went to the Supreme Court to speak out against the Indian Removal Act, and the Supreme Court agreed with them. Jackson ignored the Supreme

Court decision and ordered the removal. In 1838, more than 15,000 Cherokees were forced to leave their homes in parts of North Carolina, Georgia, Tennessee, and Alabama. They walked all the way to what is now Oklahoma. About 4,000 Cherokees died along the way. The Cherokees journey later became known as the Trail of Tears. By 1840, more than 60,000 Native Americans had been removed. The mid-1800 was an exciting time in the U.S. More and more Americans headed west. Although to move west, Americans needed to develop better ways of traveling.

Railroads

In April 1830, Peter Cooper tested his invention. It was a steam-powered train. Soon the railroad fever had spread everywhere and by the 1850's the cities of Cleveland, Detroit, Chicago, and St. Louis were all joined to the east coast by railroads.

Settling the West

There were many reasons why many Americans moved west in the 1830 and 1840's. At the end of Jackson's presidency, the economy became worse. Many banks failed, farmers and business people lost millions of dollars. For many people, moving west was a way to start over.

Americans in Texas

Americans who settled in Texas wanted to break away from Mexico. They wanted independence as well. They formed an army led by Sam Houston.

The Alamo

In 1836, a force about 200 Texans were in their fort, the Alamo. With more than 4,000 men, Santa Anna attacked the fort. The Texans fought very hard and held out for 13 days. However, the Mexicans defeated the Texans who were all killed. Santa Anna Thought his victory would stop the rebels in Texas. He was very wrong. **"Remember the Alamo!!!!"** became the battle cry of Sam Houston's men. A few months after the Alamo, the Texans defeated the Mexican Army at the battle of San Jacinto. The Texans took Santa Anna prisoner. Texas declared itself an independent nation in 1836. In 1845, Texas became the 28th state to enter the Union.

The Gold Rush

By 1849, the news of the discovery of gold spread quickly. People rushed to California.

They wanted some of the riches. The California gold rush had began. More than 70,000 people traveled to California. These people became known as the 49ers, because they went to California in 1849 to find gold.

Immigrants From Europe

Between 1830 and 1860, nearly five million immigrants came to the United States. Most of the immigrants came from the northern and western parts of Europe. Many came from Germany and Ireland.

Immigrants from Asia

In the 1840's, many immigrants came to the U.S. They came mainly to escape both political and economic problems in their country. Many of these immigrants were farmers. They were interested in starting farms on the frontier.

Women Fight for Their Right

They had very few rights that women today take for granted. Women wanted to improve their lives and the lives of others. Many women felt slavery was wrong. This gave them a reason to come together. In the 1820's and the 1830's, many women raised their voices against slavery and for equal rights. Equal rights are what all people in one society should have. These women worked very hard to gain equal rights for all U.S. Citizens. However, there were still without one important right. That was the right to vote. The right to vote is called suffrage. In 1851, Elizabeth Cady Stanton, and Susan B. Anthony met. Soon they began working together for all women's rights. In New York, Anthony and Stanton help get a law passed that protected the right of all women to own property, collect their own wages and could sue a person in a court of law and they could now enter into contracts. From that moment all other states were able to similar laws passed.

Public Education Reform

During the 1800's not all children went to school, on the very wealthy families went to school, private schools. Poor children received no education outside of home. Horace Mann wrote, *"If we do not prepare our children to become good citizens, if we do not develop their skills, if we do not enrich their minds with knowledge and fill their hearts with love of truth and duty...then our country must go down the destruction... "*

The Missouri Compromise of 1820

By 1819, there were 22 states in the U.S. of America. There were 11 free states in which slavery was not allowed. There were 11 slave states in which slavery was allowed. 1809 Missouri asked to become a state. In 1820, Maine asked to become a state as well. Missouri wanted to join the Union, or the United States as slave state. Missouri was a part of the Louisiana Territory. Northern lawmakers did not want Missouri to become a state. 12 slave states would be too much, the north and the south could not agree. In 1820, a senator named Henry Clay of Kentucky came up with an idea, a compromise. The main point of this compromise was this. 1. Missouri would enter the Union as a slave state. 2. Maine would enter the Union as a free state. 3. The rest of Louisiana Territory could be divided by a line. No slavery would be allowed in the states north of that line. As the 1830's came to an end, the nation was deeply divided over the question of slavery. The Union was in danger of breaking a part. Some people in the North wanted to abolish or end slavery. These people were called abolitionists. Fredrick Douglass was a well-known speaker and abolitionist. When he was 21 years old, Douglass made his escape. He became a leader in the Massachusetts abolitionist society. He spoke about why slavery was wrong. Douglass wrote the narrative of *The Life of Fredrick Douglass,* a book about his experiences as a slave.

The Underground Railroad

Like a real railroad, the Underground Railroad had "tracks, stations and conductors". The tracks were the secret routes started in the South and went through a number of Northern states.

The stations were secret hiding places in houses, churches and caves. About 100,000 slaves used the Underground Railroad to escape to freedom. Harriet Tubman was one famous conductor. Tubman was an escaped slave and even though she was free, Tubman returned to the South 19 times to help more than 300 enslaved African Americans to escape.

The Kansas-Nebraska Act

In 1854, Bleeding Kansas, or also known as just Kansas had two governments. One was for slavery and one was against it. Each claimed to be the legal government. Violence broke out, in May 1856; about 700 pro-slavery extremists attacked Lawrence, Kansas, which was the capital of the anti-slavery government. The attackers robbed people and destroyed property.

Several days later, an anti-slavery group murdered five pro-slavery men and boys. Bloody battles and killings began. The territory became known as "Bleeding Kansas". More than 200 people were killed.

Preparing for War

After the Confederate cannons fired on Fort Sumter in 1861, there would be no more compromises between the north and the south. The Nation continued to divide.

Battle of Bull Run

The first big battle of the war took place in July 1861, near a creek named Bull Run, in Virginia. Bull Run was only 20 miles away from Washington D.C. Members of congress and other Union supporters went to the battlefield to watch. Soldiers on both sides fought hard.

However, the Union soldiers were poorly trained. When new Confederate troops, or soldiers arrived, the Union soldiers retreated, or turned back. Union supporters began to understand that this war would not be won quickly. After Bull Run, many Southerners thought that they could win the war. In the first year of the war, the North and the South fought in the southeast, at sea and in the Mississippi River Valley. The South won some battles. The North won still yet others. Neither side could totally defeat the other. Yet, the North prevailed.

The Emancipation Proclamation

The summer of 1862, Lincoln had decided to take steps to end slavery in the Southern states that were still held by Confederacy. Lincoln thought that if the Southern slaves were freed, they would refuse to work in the fields. Then plantations would not be able to grow food for Southern troops. Lincoln also thought that freeing the slaves would help many Northerners understand why the war was important. As a result, President Lincoln issued the Emancipation Proclamation. This was a public statement that freed the enslaved African Americans in the rebelling states, and the Confederacy states would be "forever free". The Proclamation did not actually set any slaves free because the Union had no way to enforce the Proclamation. The Proclamation did not apply to the slaves in the Border States because Lincoln needed the support of these states. At about the same time, Lincoln issued the Emancipation Proclamation; he decided to allow African American soldiers to serve in the Union Army. Nearly 180,000 African Americans enlisted, or volunteered. Many of them were escaped slaves.

The 54th Massachusetts Volunteers

The best-known African American soldiers were the 54th Massachusetts volunteers. These soldiers were free African Americans. Fredrick Douglass' two sons also fought in the unit.

Colonel Robert Shaw was the officer of the unit.

Surrender at Appomattox

By the spring of 1865, the Confederacy was beaten. Its armies were running out of troops and supplies. On April 3, Union troops entered Richmond, which at that time was the Confederate capital. Lee and his men retreated until they were cornered at the village of Appomattox Court House, in central Virginia. On April 9, 1865, Lee and Grant met at the Appomattox Court House. They agreed to end the war.

Grant did not believe in punishing the South. Grant and Lee agreed to these terms of surrender: 1. Southern soldiers must give up their weapons, 2. Southern soldiers could keep their horses or mules if they owned them, 3. all Southern officers could keep their pistols, swords, and horses, 4. All Southern soldiers would be fed, 5. The South had to promise to end slavery, 6. The South had to take a loyalty oath before they could be forgiven, 7. Property, but not slaves, would be returned to the former Confederates who took the loyalty oath, and finally give blacks a right to vote.

African Americans Work to Build New Lives

The Freedmen's Bureau played an important role in starting schools for African Americans who had been enslaved. Most of the schools were elementary schools. It had been against the law to educate the slaves. By 1869, more than 300,000 slaves attended the Freedmen's Bureau Schools. African Americans and poor whites voted and held public office. It looked at though the South really was being reconstructed.

Broken Promises

The settlers and railroads changed the land as they moved west. They also changed the lives of the Native Americans who had lived there for centuries. Native Americans were forced onto land that was far from the land that they loved and knew. Many Native Americans began to fight to protect their land and traditions. In 1864, gold miners moving onto Native American land near Sand Creek, Colorado. Several hundred Cheyenne and Arapahos were settled there. Soon fighting broke out. U.S. troops attacked the Indian village at Sand Creek. The Native American Chief saw that his village was in great danger. He raised a white flag as a signal that he did not want to fight. However, the soldiers did not stop their attack. Hundreds of Native Americans, men, women and children were slaughtered. What promises that were made to the Native American people were broken at that point in time.

The Beef Business Grows

Cattle first arrived in North America with the Spanish settlers. At first, the cattle were raised for their skins. Cattle leather was used in clothing, shoes, and other good, however, as the country's population grew, more and more people began to eat beef. After the Civil War, the demand for beef increased. Cattle became very, very valuable.

The Cowhand's Life

As the beef business grew, so did the need for workers. Most cowhands were young men. They were usually in their early twenties. They worked through dust storms, blazing heat and icy blizzards. Most of the year, cowhands kept the cattle from getting lost of stolen. Once a year, cowhands went on a cattle drive. They rounded up the cattle into herds and guided them to towns where there were railroad lines. A cattle drive often lasted two to three months. Cattle drives were a difficult way to make a living. In the mid-1880's, water holes dried up and grasslands turned to dust. Blizzards that happened in 1886 and 1887 ended up killing thousands of heads of cattle. By the end of the 1880's the cowhand's way of life had all but disappeared.

Mining Town

Mining was often difficult and deadly work. Miners worked underground and in almost darkness. Poison gases, cave-ins and accidents were part of daily life there. In the 1870's, one miner out of ever 30 died.

Boomtowns

Since boomtowns grew quickly, and usually there were not law officers to be had. Thieves, outlaws and dishonest gamblers often broke the law. In many towns, citizens formed vigilante committees. These committees were groups of people who joined together to keep order and punish criminals. However, they did so without any authority. Members of vigilante committees hunted down lawbreakers. Often the vigilantes had lawbreakers hung or shot without the benefit of a trial. The mining book was over by the end of the 1800s. Much of the wealth from mining went to large mining companies.

The Machine Age

Between 1860 and 1900, the United States changed from an economy based on farming to an economy based on industry. Inventions and industry changed the way Americans lived, worked and traveled. Thomas Alva Edison probably invented more things than any other person in history. In his lifetime, Edison received 1,093 patents in the United States. This is more than any other person has ever received.

As the 1900s began, the United States faced a number of problems. They included poverty, unsafe working conditions, and unclean food. Some Americans blamed the rich people for these problems. Some Americans said capitalism did not work. Many of these people, called Progressives, thought they could improve the system by working together with the government. Progressives believed that many problems were caused by the fast growth of the industry and cities. They wanted laws to regulate and control businesses and to improve working conditions. They also felt that laws were needed to improve health and education in poor neighborhoods.

In 1904, Roosevelt was easily elected president. Roosevelt got

Congress to pass laws that cleared run-down areas of cities and made factories safer. Laws were also passed to control the power of railroads and allow health officials to inspect meatpacking plants.

The Great White Fleet

In 1907, President Theodore Roosevelt wanted to show the world that the United States was becoming a great power. He sent 16 battleships, called the Great White Fleet on a world tour. At every port, people welcomed the fleet and around the world, people could see the power of the U.S. Navy.

A Voice from the Past

With words of a famous fighter, Jose Marti, *"Let us rise up so that freedom will not be endangered by apathy. Let us rise up for the true republic, those of us who .... with our habit of hard work will know how to preserve it and let us place around the star of our new flag. "*

A World War Begins

In 1914, war broke out in Europe. The war was called the Great War. Later it was called World War I. These names showed that this war was different from earlier wars. Whole nations, including soldiers and civilians, suffered in this war. The Great War affected people all over the world. Woodrow Wilson was president at that time and wanted to keep the United States out of this war. However, Germany's actions made many Americans angry, including the President. Finally, in 1917, the United States was drawn into the war. Once the U.S. troops were trained, they had to cross the Atlantic Ocean to reach Europe. However, crossing the Atlantic was very dangerous. More than 100 German submarines moved quietly beneath the waters. To carry troops safely across the ocean, the U.S. Navy traveled in convoys. In this system, warships traveled along with the ships that carried the troops. The first American troops arrived in France in June 1917. Over the next months, more than one million U.S. soldiers came to France to fight. In early 1918, German forces planned to attack Paris, the capital of France. They broke through the Allied lines and came within 50 miles of Paris.

However, the French and U.S. troops stopped them. The American troops fought two very important battles in France that helped end the war. They were the Belleau Wood and the Argonne Forest. The U.S. had been in the war for less than a year. U.S. troops had provided the extra forces needed by the allies. Although U.S. losses were great, they were far fewer than those of other countries in that war. The war had taken a terrible toll in Europe. As many as 13 million civilians and soldiers died in that war. Much of northern France was destroyed. In Germany, millions of people were starving. Between 1918 and 1919, even more people died from a flu epidemic. The flu epidemic killed around 20 million people. In 1920, the United States had come out of World War I safely as can be. The nation was once again at peace. The economy was healthy. America was beginning to enjoy the good times.

Good Times for Many

The 1920's were a time of prosperity, or good times, and change for many people. More people enjoyed wealth and luxury. Americans lived with high hopes for the future. Cars were something new in the 1920s. There was new music as well. Families now had radios in their homes. People could go to movies and be entertained. For many people, the 1920s was simply a time to enjoy life. People called those carefree times the Roaring Twenties. Another nickname for that time was the Jazz Age.

The Great Depression

All too soon, America was rocked to its very financial foundations. On October 29, 1929, the stock market crashed. It is also known as Black Tuesday. As the 1920s close, millions of people were out of work. Farmers were losing their farms. Banks began to go out of business because they had used their customer's savings to buy stocks. By the beginning of 1932, the U.S. economy had almost fallen completely apart. Thousands of businesses had closed. 80% of all factory owners could not afford to pay their employees. Many people lost their jobs, and as a result, most Americans could not afford to buy the goods that were being made. Unsold goods began to pile up and the workers who had the jobs were paid $1.50 a day to buy the food. The Great Depression grew even worse. Many Americans lost their homes as well as their jobs. In all the major cities and even some rural areas, there were people standing in soup lines waiting for hours to be fed. Families sold apples to earn a few cents. Thousands of people who were hungry sometimes picked through garbage cans for scraps of food. The failure of the government and big businesses to help people made many Americans angry. These are some of the things that people did to express their anger. 1. Some workers without jobs joined the communist party, 2. Some farmers destroyed their crops rather than sell them at unfair prices, 3. Some farmers joined together to stop banks from taking their property, 4. Many World War I veterans marched on Washington D.C in 1932. World War I veterans were especially angry with the government. After world War I, Congress had voted to give veterans a bonus, so when the depression hit, the government then refused to pay for it. During the summer of 1932, 15,000 veterans farmed what became known as the Bonus Army.

African Americans and the Great Depression

African Americans had been among the poorest Americans for the longest time. When the depression hit, their lives became even harder. As the economy grew worse, African Americans were among the first to be fired. Many bosses lowered their pay to help save money. Many African Americans, often had the most dangerous and dirty jobs, lost their jobs to white people. By 1932, one half of all African Americans had no jobs. By 1932, about 12 million Americans were without jobs. Most were also without money and without hope. They were looking for a leader. They found that leader in Franklin D. Roosevelt. Five days after Roosevelt became president, he called a special meeting of Congress. The President and Congress began to work on his plan for the nation. Most Americans supported the President's plans; however, the Supreme Court disagreed with the President. The court felt that the President's programs gave the government too much power. They thought some new deal programs were against the Constitution. The opinion of the Supreme Court member shocked the President. He decided to do something. He said that the country needed more and younger judges. As the 1930s came to an end, many of the problems of the Great Depression still remained. However, the new laws and programs of President Roosevelt gave the government a new role in the lives of Americans. In addition, some Americans played a larger role in government than ever before.

Women had a larger part in political decisions; some even became judges. Some women also represented the United States in other countries. African Americans were given new hope by the President as well. Roosevelt called together a group that was called the Black Cabinet. Mary Mclead Bethune was a member of this group. The President asked her to serve as the head of the National Youth Administration, which helped young people, find work.

Native Americans were helped as well by the Indian Organization act of 1934. Under this act, ways were provided to help Native Americans keep their customs and ways of life. Lands were returned and thousands were given jobs on their lands. As bad as the Great Depression was, most people found ways to get through it. They even found ways to cope during the hard times.

Athletes as Heroes

Athletes were heroes to many people in the 1930s; thousands of Americans cheered such baseball players as Lou Genring, Joe DiMaggio and J. H. Dizzy Dean. Football also became a popular sport with the help of "Whizzer" White Sid Luckman, and "Bronko" Nagasaki. Some of the most admired athletes of the 1930s were African Americans. Blacks were not allowed to play major baseball. Instead, they played in the Negro leagues. African Americans cheered such players as Leroy Robert Satchel Paige and Josh Gibson. In 1932, many people wondered whether the Olympic games would be held in Los Angles. They questioned whether anyone would have the money to spend on the games. Despite the lack of money, the Games were held and people did come. In 1936, the games were held in Berlin Germany.

Adolph Hitler, the leader of Germany, was spreading anti-Semitism in his country. Hitler also believed that white athletes were much better than African American athletes. Needless to-say, runner, Jesse Owens, an African American, won four gold medals. He proved that Hitler's belief was wrong.

From Isolation to Pearl Harbor

After World War I, most Americans feared that Alliances and other nations would pull the U.S. into another war. Yet, Americans could see the growing signs of yet another war in Europe and Asia.

Many Americans asked whether the U.S. had duty to help other countries. Staying out of wars was what the American people wanted. Between 1935 and 1937 the U.S. Congress passed several laws to keep the country out of wars. Many Americans backed these laws because they wanted the U.S. to remain a peaceful nation. Just before 1940, no president had ever run for a third term, but the election of 1940 was different. The reason for this was the war in Europe. Many Americans felt Roosevelt's experience, as a leader was necessary if the United States did go to war. President Roosevelt had promised the American people that if he were elected for a third term, he would keep the United States out of the war. Soon after the election of 1940, Winston Churchill, the leader of Great Britain, asked the United States for help against Nazi Germany. Britain did not have the manpower, or enough money to buy weapons. Roosevelt was able to get Congress to agree on a lend-lease plan, but sending ships, guns and other supplies to Britain became very dangerous. German submarines began attacking American ships. In October 1941, German submarines sank a U.S. Navy ship, killing 115 sailors. To many, it seemed as if war was on the way. In September 1949, Japan became an ally of Germany and Italy. At the same time, Japan continued to expand into Asia. In protest of this, President Roosevelt, stopped all trade with Japan in September 1941. He banned oil shipments to Japan. Japan needed oil to keep its military tanks, trucks and airplanes working.

Japan and the U.S. started talks in November 1941. Neither side would compromise. While the talks continued, Japan was busy making plans to attack the U.S. Navel base in Pearl Harbor, Hawaii.

Before dawn in Hawaii on Sunday, December 7, 1941, Japanese pilots headed toward the navel base at Pearl Harbor, which was located on the Hawaiian Island of Oahu. These Japanese planes destroyed 19 American ships and killed more than 2,400 Americans. The next day,

December 8, 1941, Roosevelt asked Congress to declare war on Japan. Congress agreed, and the U.S. once again joined its allies to fight a war. In the spring of 1942, the allies began to move across the Pacific Ocean. An aircraft carrier moved within 700 miles of Japan. On the carrier there were 16 lightweight American bombers. The bombers took off from the carrier and headed for Tokyo. They flew low over Tokyo, bombing factories, railroad yards and the navy base. The Japanese were shocked. No enemy had ever attacked their homeland. After the bombings, the Japanese decided to push closer to U.S. territory. This huge Japanese fleet headed for Midway Island. The U.S. fleet sailed to meet the Japanese. At dawn on June 4, 1942, U.S. planes attacked Japanese planes. They were caught by surprise. They suffered great losses. The battle of Midway was the first big defeat for the Japanese.

Critical Thinking on the Part of U.S.

The military was losing the war and they needed something that would turn things around. The U.S. was losing men by the thousands. The government called on more than 400 Navajos, who served in the U.S. Marines and were called "code talkers" during World War II. The Navajo language worked as a code. It was difficult for anyone who was not familiar with it to understand it. Every sound in the language means something. The meaning can change if a speaker's voice is low or high. The Navajo code was never broken. It was one of the war's most secure communication systems.

During the war, women made up about one third of all factory workers. In the past, women who worked had most often been young and unmarried. By 1944, more married women than unmarried women held positions in factories. Women took on many new responsibilities.

Some of those were: 1. Women now served in the Armed Forces in greater numbers, 2. Women worked in military offices so that more men could serve in battle, 3. Women flew supply planes so that the men could fly fighters and bombers. 4. Women served as nurses. They often lived under the same dangerous conditions as the soldiers.

African Americans During the War

More than 27 million Americans moved during the war. It was the largest migration of people in U.S. history, and many African Americans moved to cities in the northeast, in the Midwest and on the west coast to work the factories. For African Americans, World War II brought many changes. Many African Americans left low-paying farm jobs in the south for better-paying factory jobs in other parts of the U.S. Roosevelt signed an order to make sure African Americans were treated fairly in defense plants. Over a million African Americans served in the armed forces during WWII. However, even in the armed forces, Negroes faced a multitude of discriminations. Those where joined the armed forces were given jobs as cooks, waiters, or workers in the supply units. In spite of this, many Negroes still wanted to be part of the fighting. In 1941, one group of the 332nd fighter group was formed. All the pilots in this division were African American. They were known as the Tuskegee Airmen. The Tuskegee airmen carried out missions, or special assignments, during that time of war. These men protected bombers flying over Europe. The fighter group shot down 103 enemy planes and destroyed 298 enemy planes on the ground. No bomber protected by these Tuskegee airmen was ever shot down. During World War II, more Latino volunteered for service than any other group in the United States. Still they faced discrimination as well, in the armed forces and at home. More than 300,000 Latinos served in the armed forces during the war. Many were Mexican Americans and Puerto Ricans. About on in four of the men on the Bataan Death March was Mexican American.

D-Day Invasion

To end the war, there had to be an Allied invasion, or an attack of a huge magnitude. For more than six months, allied troops prepared to land on the coast of Europe. General Dwight D Eisenhower of the U.S. Army planned the invasion. Later, he would lead all Allied troops to victory in Europe.

End of the War

The allies wanted to force Hitler to surrender, so they began to bomb German cities day and night. Germany's defeat seemed certain, however, the Nazis made one final attack on all the Allies in December 1944. Instead, the Allies forced German troops to retreat toward Berlin, the capital of Germany. Soon millions of allied soldiers were closing in on the German capital from all directions. Finally, on May 7, 1945, Germany surrendered. The war in Europe was finally over.

The Holocaust

Allied Troops moved into Germany and into lands that Germany had controlled. Soon they found evidence of one of the most horrible acts of the war. It was the Holocaust. The Holocaust was the mass murder and imprisoning of millions of Jews by the Nazis. During his rise to power, Hitler had blamed the Jewish people for most of Germany's problems. Before long, the Nazis decided on what they called a "final solution" for the Jews. The solution was genocide.

To do this, the Nazis built death camps, where they sent Jews from all the areas that they controlled. These death camps had specially built gas chambers. The Nazis killed thousands of people every day. Their bodies were burned in huge ovens. In all, the Nazis killed six million Jews. The Holocaust is still known today as one of the most horrific acts of violence during a war.

Helping Veterans

President Harry Truman and many other Americans wanted to help the veterans, or soldiers who had fought in the war. Veterans needed an education,jobs and housing. To help these veterans, Congress passed an act called the GI Bill of Rights. Which is still working very well in the present day.

Rock and Roll and Changes that Come

Rock and Roll had started in the 1940s and 1950s. Many African Americans moved from the south to the north and brought this new kind of music with them. It was called rhythm and blues; this kind of music mixes a jazz beat with a sad kind of music called the Blues. Radio stations in the north started playing this kind of music. Alan Freed, a white disc jockey, gave Rhythm and blues a new name. He called it Rock and Roll. Soon African Americans were recording top selling rock and roll hits. Then in 1955, a new singer by the name of Elvis Presley appeared on the scene. Like many of the African American musicians, Elvis had grown up in the south. However, Elvis was white. He became a huge rock and roll star. Elvis Presley opened the door for a new group of rock and roll musicians. Jerry Lee Lewis, Buddy Holly, and the Everly Brothers were white southerners who had made top-selling hits. Chuck Berry, an African American, wrote songs about the problems of young people. He was the first great rock and roll guitar player.

In 1952, Americans elected Dwight D. Eisenhower as their new President. Most Americans were happy with the direction in which the country was going. The Cold War, however, continued to talk much of the President's time. Eisenhower approved the building of public housing in poor city neighborhoods. He also created the departments of Health, Education and Welfare. This department ran programs on food and drug safety, health and education. The department also ran a social security program for older Americans. Eisenhower also passed the Federal Aid Highway Act. This act provided nearly $31 billion to build 41,000 miles of new highways. Thus started the interstate highway system.

The Civil Rights Movement

African Americans led the fight for equality. The first victories for civil rights were in the armed forces. Other victories were in sports and entertainment. Despite these victories, African Americans still faced discrimination in jobs, housing, and education. In the south, there was unfair laws call Jim Crow Laws. Many southern whites felt that the Jim Crow Laws were constitutional. They pointed to a decision by the U.S. Supreme Court in 1896. This decision came from a case called Plessy v Ferguson. The case was about separate railroad cars for African American and white people. The court said that "separate but equal" treatment of African Americans was legal and constitutional. However, that standing did not work well with the current thinking of most of the American public, especially the African Americans. They were tired of the "separate but equal" treatment, and knew that this ruling was very unconstitutional. After World War II, many white Americans began to disagree with the unfair treatment of the African Americans. They joined with the Negroes to work for better civil rights of equal treatment and fair laws for everyone, no matter their race, color or creed.

One of the first victories for civil rights came in the armed forces. Civil rights leaders spoke out against the segregation in the military. They wanted to integrate the military, or open it to people of all backgrounds. In 1948, President Truman signed an executive order. The order said that the military must integrate. The President's ruling made all jobs in the military open to African Americans. African Americans could serve in the same units as whites. Finally, African American officers could command white soldiers. In 1954, the defense department made an announcement. It said that there were no longer any all African American units in the military.

Fighting for an Equal Education

Since 1935, the National Association for the Advancement of Colored People had been working to end segregation. The NAACP fought hard to integrate schools. Thrugood Marshall led that fight. Marshall was the lawyer who argued the case for the African American parents and the NAACP. He told the Supreme Court judges that the idea of separate but equal was impossible. The court finally agreed. This is what Chief Justice Earl Warren wrote: *"I. The fact that a school was segregated meant that it was unequal. 2. Separate schools went against the 14th Amendment to the Constitution, which promised equal protection under the law. "* In May 1954, the Supreme Court announced its decision. The Brown v Board of Education of Topeka decision said that in public schools "separate but equal" has no place. The court said that public schools must desegregate, or end the separation of races.

The Voting Rights Act of 1965

In 1965, Congress passed the Voting Rights Act. The act said that the states could not prevent Negroes from registering to vote. The Federal Government would take over registering in any of the states that tried to stop African Americans from voting or registering to vote. By the end of the year, more than 2.5 million African Americans were registered to vote. Since then many African Americans have been elected to a political office.

Voices From the Past-Dr. Martin Luther King

Dr. Martin Luther King Jr. was one of the most influential leaders in the fight for civil rights for Blacks. He was the minister of a church in Montgomery, Alabama in the early 1950s. Later Dr. King led protests against segregation in the south. In 1963, Dr. King was arrested in Birmingham, Alabama, for leading a protest march. From jail, Dr. King wrote a letter to eight white religious leaders in Birmingham. In a Birmingham newspaper, these leaders called Dr King troublemaker. They blamed him for using "extreme measures" that lead to hatred and violence between the races. These religious thought that African Americans should work slowly for change. Dr. King answered them with his famous letter from the Birmingham jail.

Here is a portion from his letter; *"We have waited for more than 340 years for our rights ...perhaps it is easy for those who have never felt ...segregation to say WAIT! This wait has almost always meant NEVER! But when you have seen the vicious mobs lynch your mothers and fathers ...when you have seen hate-filled policemen curse, kick and even kill your black brothers and sisters ...when you are ... when you are living constantly on tip-toe stance never quite knowing what to expect next, then you will understand why we find it difficult to wait."*

The Kennedy Years

John F. Kennedy became President in January 1961. He asked the American people *"ask not what your country can do for you, but what you can do for your country. "* Kennedy had a hard time getting Congress to pass new laws. Most southern democrats in Congress did not support Kennedy's new programs. They felt Kennedy wanted to pass laws that would involve the Federal Government in business, housing and education. However, Kennedy did get some of his bills passed. These are the bills Congress voted to pass during the first months of Kennedy's term: 1. Voted to send money to places where people were jobless. 2. Voted to give money to build housing for older Americans. 3. Made it easier for young people to get loans for college.

John F. Kennedy started programs that gave Americans a chance to help others. Volunteers, or people who choose to help, took part in these programs. Some of these programs continue to help people today. Kennedy started the Peace Corps in 1961. Today nearly 6,700 volunteers work in the Peace Corps in over 77 countries around the world. After the Peace Corps, Kennedy started the Alliance for Progress in 1961, the Alliance helped people in Latin America. The volunteers helped to build homes, schools and hospitals. The Alliance lasted until 1974. In 1964, Volunteers in Service to America was organized. This group worked in neighborhoods to find ways to end poverty. Over 120,000 Americans have volunteered to work in VISTA. Congress also passed laws to control pollution. They passed laws to give more Americans social security benefits. Kennedy also got congress to approve money for Urban renewal. Kennedy helped people in other countries as well. He promised that the United States would put a man on the moon before 1970. On July 20, 1969, U.S astronauts Neil Armstrong and Edwin "Buzz" Aldrin landed on the moon.

Death of a President

On November 22, 1963, President Kennedy and Mrs. Kennedy went to Dallas, Texas. He was planning on running for a second term. Kennedy was shot dead while riding through Dallas in an open car. Later a plane carried President Kennedy's body back to Washington D.C. On that same plane, Vice President Lyndon B. Johnson was sworn in as President.

Johnson soon introduced a civil rights bill to Congress in late January 1964. Johnson worked hard to get votes for this bill. Finally Congress passed it in July. The bill became to be known as the Civil Rights Act of 1964. The Voting Rights Act was passed in 1965. President Johnson called his new ideas, goals and programs for America's future the Great Society.

Johnson wanted to help the homeless people, older Americans, low-income people and new immigrants. Johnson reached most of his goal for the Great Society.

African American Protests

By 1964, Dr. Martin Luther King Jr. was one of the most respected men in the world. His plan for nonviolent or peaceful protests had won many victories for African Americans.

However, not all African Americans agreed with Dr. King. For some, gaining fair treatment was just taking to long. Many young leaders in the fight were angry. Some believed that African Americans would be better off living separately from the whites. They spoke out against the white city officials who basically ignored their problems. They also demanded that white police officers begin to treat them fairly. One person who spoke out against the slow progress of the civil rights movement was Malcolm X. As a young black man, Malcolm X joined the black Muslims. The black Muslims believed African Americans and white Americans should live separately. In 1964, Malcolm X traveled to the city of Mecca in Saudi Arabia. There he saw that people of all races lived and worked together. When Malcolm X returned to the U.S., He spoke out against segregation. He now said that all people should work together for freedom and equality. Some African Americans did not like Malcolm X's new message. In February 1965 Malcolm X was assassinated. Three black men went to prison for his murder. In 1968, Dr. King went to Memphis, Tennessee. He planned to support a strike by African American workers. There, Dr. King spoke about the future. "I may not get there with you," he said, "but I know ... we as a people will get to the Promised Land" that was Dr. King's last speech. On April 4, 1968, he was shot as he stood on the porch of the Lorraine Motel. The death of the man who had believed in nonviolence led to riots in more than 100 cities. For many people, Dr. King's murder was the end of the Civil Rights movement.

Native Americans Call for Action

In the 1960' s living conditions on Indian Reservations were among the worst in the U.S. In 1968, the American Indian movement or AIM was formed in Minneapolis, Minnesota. Its goal was to improve the lives of Native Americans in that city. It also wanted to protect Native Americans form unfair treatment by the police. Soon there were branches of AIM in other cities. During the 1970s, AIM worked to improve schools for Native Americans and help young people on reservations understand their own culture and traditions. AIM wanted to create health care programs and get the U.S. Government to focus on the land. Native Americans finally hoped to get the government to improve conditions on the reservations.

A Distant War

Before the early 1950s, few Americans had ever heard of Vietnam. The United States had hardly any contact with that small country in Southeast Asia. Vietnam was more than 10,000 miles away. France controlled Vietnam for many years. In 1946, the people of Vietnam fought a war against France. They wanted independence. Ho Chi Mien was the man at the time and he was also a communist. In May 1954, Ho Chi Mien's forces won a great victory over the French. The war ended two months later. They won their independence. According to the pace treaty, Vietnam was divided into two parts. The North and the South., national elections were to be held in 1956. The people of Vietnam would vote for one leader to bring the country together. Ho Chi Mien took over North Vietnam. He set up a communist government there.

Ngo Dinh Diem became the leader of South Vietnam. He was against communism. The U.S. worried about that and the American leaders felt that if he won, that would be bad for the whole world. All of Vietnam as communist controlled country would be dangerous. Vietnam would take over neighboring countries, and they would become communist controlled. Vietnam was indeed a threat to all of Asia.

In 1957, people who were against Diem formed a group called the Viet Cong. They were South Vietnamese communists. In 1959, the Viet Cong joined the North Vietnamese army to fight Diem's forces. This was the beginning of the war. When John F. Kennedy became President in 1961, he continued helping South Vietnam. He sent military advisors to South Vietnam to train the South Vietnamese fighters. Fighting the Viet Cong was not easy. Viet Cong used guerrilla warfare, and they were very good at it. As the fighting continued, Diem became more and more unpopular. In 1963, South Vietnamese military leaders decided to depose Diem. On November 1, 1963, his own generals killed Diem. Three weeks later, President Kennedy was assassinated. Lyndon Johnson, the Vice President at the time, became President. Johnson believed that it was important for the U.S. to fight communism in Vietnam. He believed that North Vietnam could be defeated if the U.S. Helped South Vietnam. The question of how to fight communism was not going to be easy. The Vietnam War took an important tum in August 1964. On August 2, a U.S. warship reported that North Vietnamese gunboats had attacked it. IT was in the Gulf of Ton kin, off the coast of North Vietnam.

President Johnson spoke on television to the American people about what had happened. He described the attack. He said that American forces would fight back. Johnson asked Congress to give him the power to order U.S. forces into South Vietnam. Congress allowed Johnson to do just that.

The Ton Kin Gulf Resolution was passed on August 7, from then on; the President could send troops to Vietnam with out declaring war. In 1964, President Johnson won landslide victories in the election. He defeated Barry Goldwater, who was the republican candidate at that time. Johnson now had been elected President on his own. The American people liked Johnson's strong stand against Communism. Johnson had promised that American soldiers would not be sent to Vietnam. However, while Johnson was making his promise, plans were being made to bomb North Vietnam. So, in February 1965, Viet Cong forces attacked a military base in South Vietnam, eight Americans were killed. After that attack, Johnson ordered the bombing of North Vietnam to begin. For more than three years, the U.S. dropped 500 tons of bombs a day on North Vietnam. The bombs destroyed many areas in North Vietnam. However, it made the North Vietnamese and the Viet Cong want more than ever to continue their fight against the U.S. Many Americans supported the President's actions.

However, many Americans knew that Johnson had gone against his promises. He continued to send soldiers to Vietnam. By June, 50,000 U. S. Troops were now in Vietnam. Each day thousands of U.S troops were killed or wounded. Yet winning the war did not seem near. The U.S. was being pulled deeper and deeper into an unpopular war. Johnson knew by 1966, that this war would not end soon. This enemy was not like any other we had ever faced. To find the Viet Cong, we had to use two types of weapons that were dropped form planes One was napalm, a sticky gasoline Jelly that is used in bombs. These bombs killed plants and also it would stick to flesh. The other was Agent Orange. This stuff was the most powerful chemical used by the U.S. Nothing could survive Agent Orange. Napalm was put into bombs and dropped in areas where they could not easily reach the Viet Cong. These bombs killed or injured millions of Vietnamese. By the end of 1966, there were more than 385,000 American troops in Vietnam. Yet the Viet Cong seemed more determined than ever to win. In 1968, the Viet Cong, South Vietnamese, and the U.S. agreed to stop fighting briefly. Most South Vietnamese troops went on holiday leave. During one night, sounds of firecrackers, laughter and song filled the air in Saigon, which was the capital city of South Vietnam. Then suddenly, there was the sound of rifle fire. The Viet Cong had made a surprise attack. The Viet Cong also struck nearby South Vietnamese towns and villages. The U.S. Embassy in Saigon and a U.S. military base were also badly damaged. About 84,000 Viet Cong and North Vietnamese troops took part in what became knows and the TET offensive. People back home watching the news on TV were shocked and angry.

Much of what Americans learned about the Vietnam War came from what they saw on TV. For several years, they had been hearing that the U.S. forces were slowly winning the war in Vietnam. Americans now saw that things were much worse than they had been led to believe. Enemy forces were no longer hiding in the country and were fighting in the thick forests. They were attacking cities, towns and villages in Vietnam. After the TET Offensive, many Americans stopped supporting the war. However, some Americans believed that it was important for the U.S. to stop communism anywhere it spread. They believed that the Soviet Union and Chinese communists controlled Ho Chi Mien. They would hurt the U.S. All U.S. troops left

Vietnam by the end of March 1973. Without the United States support, the south Vietnamese forces were soon defeated. Two years later, the North Vietnamese took over Saigon. Vietnam became a country under communist rule. The veterans returning home from the war were treated badly by many of the American people. Many veterans felt that the Americans who protested the war did not respect the sacrifices that they had made. IT was not until the 1980s that the American people recognized the courage and sacrifice of the men and women who had served in Vietnam. In 1982, the Vietnam Veteran's Memorial was built. As the Vietnam War came to an end, Richard Nixon, who was the President at the time, turned his attention to other world problems. He searched for ways to have better relations with other countries. China and the U.S. had been enemies for nearly 20 years. China had hinted that it wanted to improve their relations with the U.S. and Nixon agreed that it was time for the two countries to become friends. In 1972, Nixon became the first President to visit China while in office. This friendship with China worried the Soviet Union. The Soviet Union leaders feared that the United States and China might somehow work against them. So the Soviet Union decided to try to improve relations with the U.S. In May 1972, a few months after returning from China, Nixon went to the Soviet Union. No President had ever visited the Soviet Union. Nixon met with the Soviet leader Leonid Brezhnev and agreed to limit the number of new weapons being built. Nixon made other trips to Communist countries, which made him popular in the U.S.

Nixon put into action the policy of Affirmative Action, that President Johnson had ordered in 1965. This Affirmative Action program increased opportunities in employment and education for minorities and women. Some businesses, schools and government agencies had kept women, Blacks, Hispanics and other people out.

Now they were required to give everyone the same opportunities. After Nixon resigned, Gerald Ford became the President.

In 1976, Jimmy Carter was the Democratic Party's candidate for President; some Americans felt that Ford should not have Pardoned Nixon. They also blamed Ford for the poor economy. In 1976, Carter defeated Ford in a close Election. One of Carter's first acts was to pardon young men who had avoided the draft during the Vietnam War. In addition, he created the Department of Education and the Department of Energy. He named women, Latinos, and African Americans to his cabinet and staff. He also named several women as judges. During Carter's first year, the economy improved. Inflation and joblessness increased again. In foreign policy, Carter had strong ideas. Carter believed that all nations should give human rights to their citizens. Human rights are the basic freedoms that all people should have.

Carter's biggest success in foreign policy was with Israel and Egypt. In 1978, President Carter helped bring the countries of Egypt and Israel together to make an important agreement. Anwar El-Sadat was the leader of Egypt and Menachem Begin was the leader of Israel. These two leaders and Carter met at Camp David, in Maryland. Begin and Sadat signed the Camp David Accords. It said that Egypt would enter into a peaceful relations and trade with Israel.

Israel would remove troops from land that belonged to Egypt. The Camp David Accord could not bring peace in the Middle East. However, it was a step in the right direction, toward ending years of hatred. When Ronald Reagan became President, the U.S. faced serious problems. The nation faced high inflation, a recession and high unemployment. Relations with other countries were now at a very low point. Reagan had a gift for talking to the American people. He often told stories from his past. Reagan came to be called the"Great Communicator". Two months after Reagan took office, a disturbed man named John Hinckley Jr. tried to kill him. James Brady, Reagan's Press Secretary was also shot. Reagan, having good humor after the shooting won the hearts of many of Americans. Since Reagan was republican, he said to his surgeons, "Please tell me you're republican." Reagan recovered after the shooting, however, James Brady never walked again without help. In 1988, the republicans chose George H.W. Bush, who was Reagan's vice president at the time, to run for president. Jesse Jackson, who was a civil rights leader from Chicago, ran against him and won several democratic primaries. During the election campaign, Bush said that Dukakis, the democratic candidate, had been"soft" on crime. Bush promised again and again not to raise taxes,"read my lips" he said,"No new taxes".

The next president, at the age of 46, Clinton was the youngest President since John F Kennedy. During his presidency, Clinton's personal life and past business dealings were major concerns. Yet Clinton could make people feel good about themselves, many Americans believed him when he said," I fell your pain," Under Clinton, the economy improved.

Unemployment and inflation stayed low. In 1997, Clinton and Congress agreed to a plan to balance the budget by 2002. In 1998 there was a budget surplus.

The Persian Gulf War

In the 1980's, Iran and Iraq, two countries in the Persian Gulf, fought against each other.

Saddam Hussein, the leader of Iraq, in 1990, sent 100,000 troops to invade Kuwait. He wanted to make Kuwait and its oil fields part of Iraq. It only took a few hours for Hussein to gain control of Kuwait. Bush was afraid that Iraq would invade Saudi Arabia next. Bush formed a coalition of nations that disagreed with the actions of Iraq.

The coalition sent troops, to the Middle East to help protect Saudi Arabia. This mission was called Operation Desert Shield. The United Nations warned Hussein that Iraqi troops had to go, leave Kuwait by January 15, 1991, or the United Nations would have to use "all necessary means" to remove them. Saddam Hussein did not remove his troops from Kuwait. Bush asked Congress for permission to go to war with Iraq. On January 17, 1991, the Allies attacked Iraq from the air. The allies, bombed military targets in Iraq. Most of Iraq's air force was destroyed. On February 24, a ground war began. U.S. and Coalition forces smashed through Iraqi lines. On February 27, Bush issued a cease-fire or an order to stop fighting. 540,000 U.S. Forces served in the Gulf war, 40,000 of them were women. 150 Americans were killed in that war. Later, many suffered serious health problems called the Gulf War Syndrome. 100,000 Iraqis were killed. At present, the U.S. still faced challenges from conflicts and changes in other countries. Since the 1980's, some of these problems included civil wars in Asia, the Middle East, Africa and Europe. During the 1980s and 1990s, the U.S. used sanctions, or punishments, to try and make countries change their way of thinking and acting. Americans protested Apartheid in South Africa for many years. Finally in 1986, the U.S. government used sanctions on U.S. companies doing business with South Africa. In 1990, Mandela became president of South Africa. The United Stats and South Africa began to rebuild their relationship. The 1980s and 1990s were a time of gain and losses in American society. The gap between rich and poor people became wider. Throughout the 1990s, the number of homeless people grew. However, many groups gained rights and opportunities, they had never had before and that was equality.

During the 1980s, the government cut back on programs to help women, poor people and minorities. However, during the 1980s, and

1990s many African Americans, Latinos, Native Americans and other minorities entered politics and gained political offices. There were several "firsts" Douglas Wilder of Virginia became the first African American governor. In 1992, Ben Night Nose Campbell became the first Native American U.S. Senator in more than 60 years.

Also in 1992, Nydia Velasquez became the first Puerto Rican woman elected to Congress. In the 1980s, African Americans were determined to make the birthday of Martin Luther King Jr. a national holiday. In 1994, President Clinton declared a Federal holiday in honor of King's birthday. In the 1990s, new programs and law changed lives of millions of people in the U.S.

Americans with Disabilities Act

In 1990, people with disabilities worked for a law that would give them equal rights. This law made more buildings and transportation accessible to people with disabilities. Millions of Americans did not have health insurance. President Clinton, however, won passage of some laws that affected medical care. One law provided health care for children. Another gave millions of workers the right to stay home to care for babies of sick family members.

Fighting Violence

During the 1990's, there were violent events in government buildings, schools, and at businesses. At this time, Americans saw the first major acts of terrorism inside the United States. In 1993, a bomb in 1995 killed 168 people at the Federal Building in Oklahoma City. Terrorism made Americans sad and angry. Schools and government buildings had to increase security. In 1993, the Brady Bill was passed. President Clinton and Congress did pass laws to put more police officers in all communities. President Clinton asked Maya Angelou to write a poem for his inauguration in 1993. The poem Angelou wrote was on the pulse of the morning. *"Lift up your eyes upon this day breaking for your. Give birth again to the dream. Women, children, men, take it into the palms of your hands. Mold it into the shape of your most private needs. Sculpt it onto the image of your most public self Lift up your hearts. Each new hour holds new chances for a new beginning."*

Computers

The first computers were built during the 1940s. They were developed mainly for scientist, engineers, and for military use. The early computer was called ENIAC. It weighed 30 tons and was at large as a railroad car. Today's computers can now fit in the palm of your hang. With the coming of computers, it has changed the way people communicate. The Internet also changed the way people get information, and thus the work place changed because of computers. Jobs are done differently. For many jobs today, a person must know how to use a computer. The computer has also changed where people can work. Each year, more and more people work on computers from home.

Technology in Space

Many inventions that we use every day were developed for use in space. Nonstick pots and pans, cordless vacuum cleaners and scratch resistant plastic eyeglasses were first developed for use m space.

"What an inspirational journey, what a story. I see that you enjoyed it. Yes, I did! So many, many people died. Yes, freedom came with a price. Not only for us but also for the whole world. Now that you have witnessed the beginning to the present, how do you feel about the flags, and what does it mean to you? First thing, I feel blessed to be an American, and it means just what Concord and Lexington meant, what Bunker Hill meant. It means that

the constitution for our people helped organize for justice, for liberty and for happiness. Under this banner rode Washington and his armies. Before it Burgoyne laid down his arms, it waved on the highland at West Point. When Arnold would have surrendered these fortresses and precious legacies, his night was turned into day and his treachery was driven away by beams of light from this starry banner. It cheered our army, driven out form around New York, and in their painful pilgrimages, this banner steamed in light over the soldiers' heads at Valley Forge and at Morristown. It crossed the waters rolling with ice at Trenton, and when its stars gleamed in the morning with a victory, a new day of hope dawned in the despondent nation. Our flag carries American ideas, history, and feelings and new beginnings. With the glorious revolution of 1688-89, and the nine former colonies reestablished their separate identities in 1689. Tell me more.

The First Flag

At the time of the signing of the Declaration of Independence, July 4, 1776, the United States had no official national flag. The grand union flag has historically been referred to as the "first national flag" although it has never had any official status. George Washington used it throughout the American revolutionary war. This flag did however, became the basis for the design of the first official U.S. flag. The origins of the design of the grand Union flag, closely resembles the British East India Company flag of the same era.

The Flag Resolution

On June 14, 1777, the Marine Committee of the Second Continental Congress passed the Flag Resolution with stated that the flag of the U.S. be thirteen stripes, alternating red and white, that the Union be thirteen stars, white in a blue field, representing a new constellation. The origin of the stars and stripes is likely that Francis Hopkinson of

New Jersey, a signer of the declaration of Independence, designed the 1777 flag while he was the chairman of the Continental Navy Board Middle Dept. It was designed between his appointment to the position in November 1776 and the time the Flag Resolution was adapted in June 1977. In 1795, the number of stars and stripes was increased from 13 to 15 to reflect as was stated the entry of Vermont and Kentucky as states of the Union. For a time the flag was not changed at all. IT was the 15 stars and striped flag that inspired Francis Scott Key to write the **"Star Spangled Banner"** which is now the national anthem.

In 1777 despite the resolution, a number of flags only loosely based on the prescribed design were used in the early years of American independence. Some examples are the Betsy Ross flag, Betsy Ross was an American woman said to have sewn the first American Flag, though many details of her life are conjecture. However, we do hold that she was commissioned to sketch and sew the flag. As well as Rebecca Young, who also has credit as having made the first flag, however, there is no evidence that supports this theory. However, Young's daughter Mary was said to have made the Star Spangled Banner Flag. Yet another example, the Flag Resolution, did not specify any particular arrangement, number of points, or the specific placement of stars. The pictured flag shows 13 outwardly oriented five-pointed stars arranged in a circle, the design itself is the oldest version of any U.S. flag to appear on any physical relic.

Popular designs at the time were varied and most were individually crafted rather than mass produced. Still other examples of the 13 star arrangements can be found on the Francis Hopkinson flag. The Cowpens flag, and the Brandywine flag. Despite the 1777 resolution, a number of flags only loosely based on the prescribed design were used in the early years of American independence. Like the Guilford courthouse flag, traditionally believed to have been carried by the

American troops at the battle of Gulf Court House in 1781. On April 4, 1818, a plan was passed by congress at the suggestion of U.S. Navel Captain Samuel C. Reed, in which the flag was changed to have 20 stars, with a new star to be added when each new state was admitted, but the number of stripes would remain at 13 to honor the original colonies.

The following table depicting the various/fogs designs of the United States

1775, America's first national flag- 0 stars, 13 stripes duration 18 months 1776, Battle of Bennington Military Flag, duration 1 year

1777, Betsy Ross Flag, duration 1 year

1777, Most popular Flag of the original 13 stars, duration 18 years

1795, The 15 stars and stripes for the 15 states, duration 23 years

1818, 20 stars, 13 stripes, duration 1 year

1819, 21 stars, 13 stripes duration 3years

1822, 24 stars, 13 stripes, duration 14years

1836, 25 stars, 13 stripes, duration 1 year

1837, 26 stars, 13 stripes, duration 8 years

1845, 27 stars, 13 stripes, duration 1 year

1846, 28 stars, 13 stripes, duration l year

1847, 29 stars, 13 stripes, duration 1 year

1848, 30 stars, 13 stripes, duration 3 years

1851, 31 stars, 13 stripes, duration 7 years

1858, 32 stars, 13 stripes, duration 1 year

1859, 33 stars, 13 stripes, duration 2 years

1861, 34 stars, 13 stripes, duration 2 years

1863, 35 stars, 13 stripes, duration 2 years

1865, 36 stars, 13 stripes, duration 2 years

1867, 37 stars, 13 stripes, duration 10 years

Chart Continued

1877, 38 stars, 13 stripes, duration 13 years

1890, 43 stars, 13 stripes duration 1 year

1891, 44 stars, 13 stripes, duration 5 years

1896, 45 stars, 13 stripes, duration 12 years

1908, 46 stars, 13 stripes, duration 4 years

1912, 48 stars, 13 stripes, duration 47 years

1959, 49 stars, 13 stripes duration 1 year

1960, 50 stars, 13 stripes, duration 48 years to present

Not having made any official design until 1777, a number of flags carried into battle by American forces. Even after, the vague wording of the Flag Resolution of 1777, have led to many designs. These battle flags are in honor of all the military members, past and present, who have served and are now serving our nation in times of war and peace. This display of flags is primarily for the education and information of teachers, students, and the general public, to help better understand the history of our military battles and their services to our nation.

The American Flag

The American Flag carries American ideas, history and feelings. Beginning at the colonies and coming to present time, in its sacred heraldry, in its glorious insignia has gathered and stored chiefly this supreme idea; divine right of liberty in man. Every means liberty, every thread, means liberty, every form of star and beam of stripes of light mean liberty, not lawlessness, but organized institutional liberty, liberty through laws and laws for liberty! The MIA/POW flag is to honor those still missing in action and/or POW. It is believed that theirs is no more living MIA/POW in captivity.

This next set of flags represents the major conflicts that our nation has been involved in, from WWII to present.

Iraq Freedom flag, in honor of those fighting for the freedom of the Iraq people The Afghanistan flag, to honor our troops fighting in Afghanistan

Flag of Bosnia, this flag was raised during the liberation of Bosnia

These are the three countries where our military is presently serving under combat conditions. The Desert Storm Flag, which still covers the present conflict in Iraq and Afghanistan.

Congress has not terminated the Desert Storm action period.

The Flag of South Vietnam for the country of South Vietnam at the time. It is the flag under which most of the people of our Asian community lived under at that time. It is authorized by proclamation to be used here to represent the country of South Vietnam at that time in history. The Vietnam Veterans War Commemorative Flag, which shows the map of South Vietnam, and the major units involved in the war action. This period from 1955 through1976 covered all areas of Southeast Asia.

The Korean War Commemorative flag, the Korean War was a police action, from 1950 through 1953, which has not yet ended, with our military still serving in Korea today. The last flag of this group; The WWII Commemorated Flag. Our military are still serving under NATO in Europe, and in other areas of the world from the action of WWII.

Flags of the Armed Forces in the order of their conception by Congress

The United States Army Flag

The United States Marines Flag

The United States Merchant Marines Flag, all authorized in 1776

The United States Navy Flag was authorized much later and

they were privateers until they were placed under the Department of Defense as an Armed Service.

The United States Army Air Corps Flag, this flag was part of United States Army Flag until about 1948, when it became the United States Air Force Flag.

The United States Coast Guard did not come under the department of defense until after WWII, the state flag was used to represent the National Guard, the reserves, and also the State Veterans Commission. This group of flags represents the Veterans Service Organizations. The Purple Hearts Flag was established by general George Washington, in 1782, and is the oldest organization. The Veterans of Foreign Wars was first established in 1899, and is for Veterans who served in time of war overseas or outside the U.S. The American Legion was established in 1919, and is for veterans who served during a time of war. The Disabled American Veterans was established in 1920, for all veterans who have received injuries or acquired medical conditions as a result of service in the military. These three organizations became very active as a result of service WWII. The American GI Forum was established in Texas in 1948, after a Hispanic Veteran was refused burial in a regular cemetery. Texas was the first state to pass a law authorizing all veterans of color to be buried in any cemetery. Now all states have such laws. Next, the AM. Vets, or the American Veterans Flag was established for all American veterans from all periods. (This flag is not yet provided), the veterans of Vietnam War, VVNW, became the Vietnam Veterans Coalition, and is now for all Veterans, past and present, and all active duty military of all periods. The Vietnam Veterans of Americans established in 1979, is for veterans who served in South East Asia are during the Vietnam War Period. The United States Retired is for U.S. Army Personnel who are fully retired from the army either medically or with 20 years active service. The United States Navy retired or

Fleet Command is for all Marines, Navy, Merchant Marines, and Coast Guard personnel retired from those services. The United States Air Force Retired is for all personnel retired from the U.S. Air Force. The last flag is a Historical Society Flag representing the Sons of the Confederate Veterans, which was organized in 1896, to represent and preserve the historic period of 1861 through 1865. (Men who relied on somebody else to take care of him or her did not build this country. Men who relied on themselves, who dared to shape their own lives, who had enough courage to blaze new trails, with enough confidence in them, built it.)

Personal Flags

Officers with certain billets, as well as generals and admirals, have a personal flag assigned to represent their authority and for command: these flags are usually displayed within the owner's office or raised on secondary flagstaff near the unit colors: unique flags are given to our President, Vice President, Secretary of Defense, (Army, Navy, and Air Force) the chairman of the Joint Chiefs of Staff and the Chief of each service branch. In addition, the Navy will display the flag of the Secretary of State where he or she is embarked as the Representative of the United States. The Coast Guard, being part of the Department of Homeland Security will utilize the Secretary's flag much like the Navy will utilize the Secretary of Defense's. Finally other flags are traditionally associated with the Military.

1. The most commonly carried flag was the Grand Union Flag
2. The Gadsden flag was created from a political cartoon; the Continental Marines carried it into the battle.
3. The Serapes Flag was flown from the serapes due to the loss of the traditional ensign during its capture.
4. The Cowpens's flag was depicted as being carried by the 3rd

Maryland Regiment at the Battle of Cowpens.

5. The Bennington flag is commonly to have been carried by American troops at the Battle of Bennington

6. The Guilford Courthouse flag was carried by the North Carolina Militia at the Battle of Guilford Court House

7. Several versions of the Flag of New England were carried by New England Militias, especially noted at the Battle of Bunker Hill

8. The Pine Tree Flag found some limited used as jack by early Navel vessels and boats.

9. The Bedford Flag was one of the first battle standards of the American Military

10. The Brandywine flag was carried by the 7th Pennsylvania Regiment at the Battle of Brandywine

11. The 2nd Canadian Regiment carried their flag into battle when fighting for the Continental Army.

12. The Commander-in-Chiefs Guard carried a unique banner while they protected General Washington

13. Flag of the Green Mountain Boys was the battle color of Green Mountain Boys and the Vermont Republic prior to its admission to the Union

14. A flag proclaiming "Come and Take it" was fashioned by Texans at the battle of Gonzales

15. The brief existence of Confederate States of American yielded the creation of several flags used by the Confederate Army and Navy

16. The Fort Sumter Flag gain significance for its unique canton and its lowering at the Battle of Fort Sumter.

17. Old Glory gained fame in the story of Captain William Driver keeping it safe from Confederate capture and

eventually became the nickname for the Flag of the United States itself.

The United States National Guard uses a unique flag in addition to the Air Force flag.

Although we may not know all of the people who influenced the creation and design of these flags, however, these flags themselves have influenced great patriotism and continue to do so to this day.

What does the colors of the Flags mean?

The most logical explanation for the colors of the American flag, for me, personally, it was modeled after the first unofficial American Flag, the Continental Colors. The colors were designed using the colors of Great Britain's Union Jack. The colors of the Great Seal are the same as the colors in the American Flag.

The Meaning to these Colors

The colors symbolize the patriotic ideals and spiritual qualities of its citizens. The vertical stripes are those used in the flag of the United States of America; the white stands for liberty and equality for all people. The blue stands for loyalty, faith and the blue of heaven. Red proclaims the fearless courage and integrity, blood and sacrifice of eternal principles: liberty, justice and humanity. The stars in the field of blue represent a new constellation, a new nation dedicated to our personal, religious liberty of all mankind, and the broad band above the stripes, is justice, perseverance and justice.

Flag Etiquette

The United States flag should never be dipped to any person or thing, this flag dips to no man or early king. The flag must never touch the ground, and if flown at night, must be illuminated. If the edges become tattered through wear, the flag should be repaired or replaced. If the flag becomes to tattered that is can no longer serve, as a symbol of the United States, burning should destroy it in a dignified manner, preferably.

Significantly, the flag should not be embroidered, printed or otherwise impressed on such articles as cushions, handkerchiefs, napkins, boxes, or anything intended to be discarded after temporary use. The United States flag is more than symbolic, it is an American Legacy, it is the secret of that something, which stamped Americans as Americans. Some call it individual initiative, others backbone, but whatever it is called, it is a precious ingredient in our national character, the flag echoes of democracy in a republic sovereign nation of many sovereign states; a perfect union, one and inseparable; established upon these principals of freedom, equality, justice and humanity for which American patriots sacrificed their lives and fortunes. When you look at our flag and behold it emblazoned with all our rights, we must remember that is it equally a symbol of our duties. Every glory that we associated with it is the result of duty done. Contemplation of our flag daily strengthens and purified the nations conscience.

Appendix

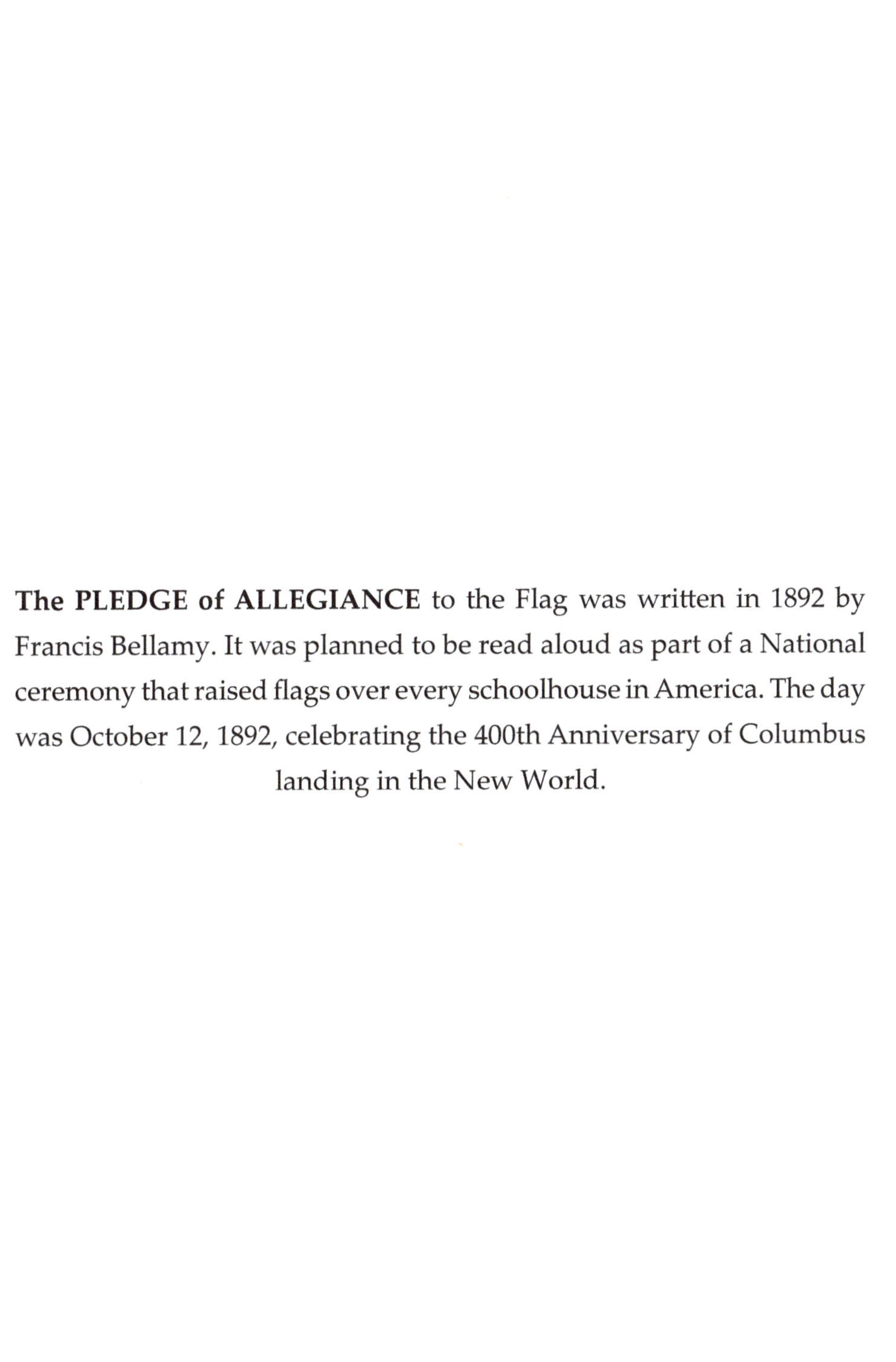

The PLEDGE of ALLEGIANCE to the Flag was written in 1892 by Francis Bellamy. It was planned to be read aloud as part of a National ceremony that raised flags over every schoolhouse in America. The day was October 12, 1892, celebrating the 400th Anniversary of Columbus landing in the New World.

We do honor the American Flags and the stars and stripes, as the emblem of our country and the symbol of all that our patriotism means. We all identify the flags with everything we hold dear on this earth. It represents our peace and security, our civil and political liberty, our freedom of religious worship, our family our friends, our home. We see it in the great multitude of blessings, of rights and privileges that make up our country. And when we look at our flag and behold it emblazoned with all our rights, we must remember that it is equally a symbol of our duties. Every glory that we associate with it is the result of duty done. A yearly contemplation of our flag strengthens and purifies the national conscience.

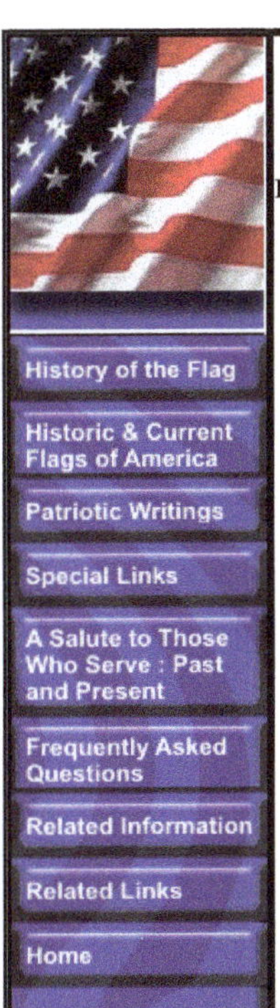

Site Key: Click to Listen Click to Print *Search:* GO

Confederate Stars and Bars

Civil War Era Flags pictured on this page are available for purchase from my friends at U.S. Flag Depot, Inc.

The First Official Flag of the Confederacy. Although less well known than the "Confederate Battle Flags",the Stars and Bars was used as the official flag of the Confederacy from March 1861 to May of 1863. The pattern and colors of this flag did not distinguish it sharply fom the Stars and Stripes of the Union. Consequently, considerable confusion was caused on the battlefield.

The seven stars represent the original Confederate States; South Carolina (December 20, 1860), Mississippi(January 9, 1861), Florida (January 10,1861), Alabama (January 11, 1861), Georgia (January 19, 1861), Louisiana (January 26, 1861), and Texas (February 1, 1861).

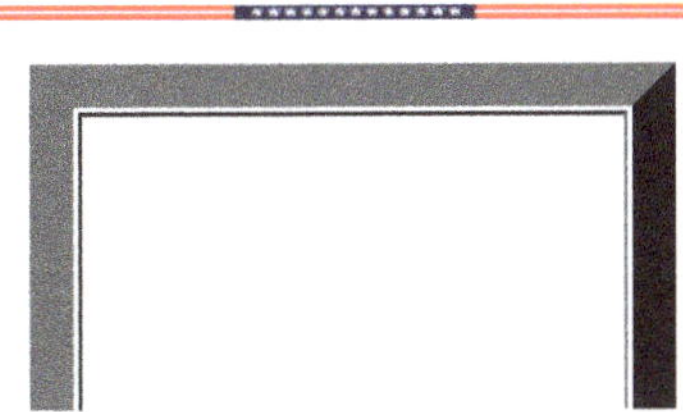

History of the Flag

Historic & Current Flags of America

Patriotic Writings

Special Links

A Salute to Those Who Serve : Past and Present

Frequently Asked Questions

Related Information

Related Links

Home

The Confederate Battle Flag. The best-known Confederate flag, however, was the Battle Flag, the familiar "Southern Cross". It was carried by Confederate troops in the field which were the vast majority of forces under the confederacy.
The Stars represented the 11 states actually in the Confederacy plus Kentucky and Missouri.

The second Official Flag of the Confederacy. On May 1st,1863, a second design was adopted, placing the Battle Flag (also known as the "Southern Cross") as the canton on a white field. This flag was easily mistaken for a white flag of surrender especially when the air was calm and the flag hung limply.

The flag now had 13 stars having been joined officially by four more states, Virginia (April 17, 1861), Arkansas (May 6, 1861), Tennessee (May 7, 1861), North Carolina (May 21, 1861). Efforts to secede failed in Kentucky and Missouri though those states were represented by two of the stars.

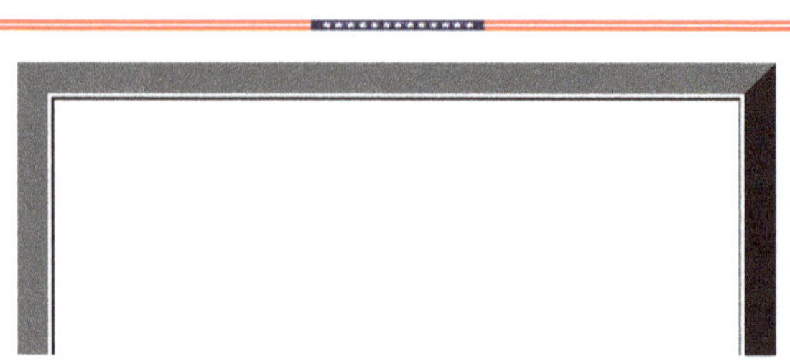

The third Official Flag of the Confederacy.On March 4th,1865, a short time before the collapse of the Confederacy, a third pattern was adapted; a broad bar of red was placed on the fly end of the white field.

Confederate Navy Jack: Used as a navy jack at sea from 1863 onward. This flag has become the generally recognized symbol of the South.

Note: It is necessary to disclaim any connection of these flags to neo-nazis, red-necks, skin-heads and the like. These groups have adopted this flag and desecrated it by their acts. They have no right to use this flag - it is a flag of honor, designed by the confederacy as a banner representing state's rights and still revered by the South. In fact, under attack, it still flies over the South Carolina capitol building. The South denies any relation to these hate groups and denies them the right to use the flags of the confederacy for any purpose. The crimes committed by these groups under the stolen banner of the conderacy only exacerbate the lies which link the seccesion to slavery interests when, from a Southerner's view, the cause was state's rights.

Note contributed by BJ Meksikatsi.

Farewell to the Army of Northern Virginia

by Robert E. Lee

After four years of arduous service, marked by unsurpassed courage and fortitude, the Army of Northern Virginia has been compelled to yield to overwhelming numbers and resources.

I need not tell the survivors of so many hard-fought battles who have remained steadfast to the last that I have consented to this result from no distrust of them; but feeling that valor and devotion could accomplish nothing that could compensate for the loss that would have attended the continuance of the contest, I determined to avoid the useless sacrifice of those whose past services have endeared them to their countrymen. By the terms of the agreement, officers and men can return to their homes and remain until exchanged.

You may take with you the satisfaction that proceeds from the consciousness of duty faithfully performed, and I earnestly pray that a merciful God will extend to you his blessing and protection.

With an unceasing admiration of your constancy and devotion to your country, and a grateful remembrance of your kind and generous consideration of myself, I bid you all an affectionate farewell.

The Character of Lee

by John Williams Jones

He possessed every virtue of the great commanders, without their vices. He was a foe without hate; a friend without treachery; a private citizen without wrong; a neighbor without reproach; a Christian without hypocrisy, and a man without guilt. He was a Caesar without his ambition; a Frederick without his tyranny; a Napoleon without his selfishness; and a Washington without his reward. He was obedient to authority as a servant, and loyal in authority as a true king. He was gentle as a woman in life; modest and pure as a virgin in thought; watchful as a Roman vestal in duty; submissive to law as Socrates, and grand in battle as Achilles.

He Lost a War and Won Immortality

by Louis Redmond

Even among the free, it is not always easy to live together. There came a time, less than a hundred years ago, when the people of this country disagreed so bitterly among themselves that some of them felt they could not go on living with the rest.

A test of arms was made to decide whether Americans should remain one nation or become two. The armies of those who believed in two nations were led by a man named Robert E. Lee.

What about Lee? What kind of man was he who nearly split the history of the United States down the middle and made two separate books of it?

They say you had to see him to believe that a man so fine could exist. He was handsome. He was clever. He was brave. He was gentle. He was generous and charming, noble and modst, admired and beloved. He had never failed at anything in his upright soldier's life. He was a born winner, this Robert E. Lee. Except for once. In the greatest contest of his life, in the war beween the South and the North, Robert E. Lee lost.

Now there were men who came with smouldering eyes to Lee and said: "Let's not accept this result as final. Let's keep our anger alive. Let's be grim and unconvinced, and wear our bitterness like a medal. You can be our leader in this."

But Lee shook his head at those men. "Abandon your animosities," he said, "and make your sons Americans."

And what did he do himself when his war was lost? He took a job as president of a tiny college, with forty students and four profes- sors, at a salary of $1500 a year. He had commanded thousands of young men in battle. Now he wanted to prepare a few hun- dred of them for the duties of peace. So the countrymen of Robert E. Lee saw how a born winner loses, and it seemed to them that in defeat he won his most lasting victory.

There is an art of losing, and Robert E. Lee is its finest teacher. In a democracy, where opposing viewpoints regularly meet for a test of ballots, it is good for all of us to know how to lose occasionally, how to yield peacefully, for the sake of freedom. Lee is our master in this. The man who fought against the Union showed us what unity means.

This page is maintained by Duane Streufert, Contact Us.
Questions or comments welcome!
This Site Established on 20 November 1994.
Last Updated 10 February 2005.
Web Design and Development by Visionary Enterprises

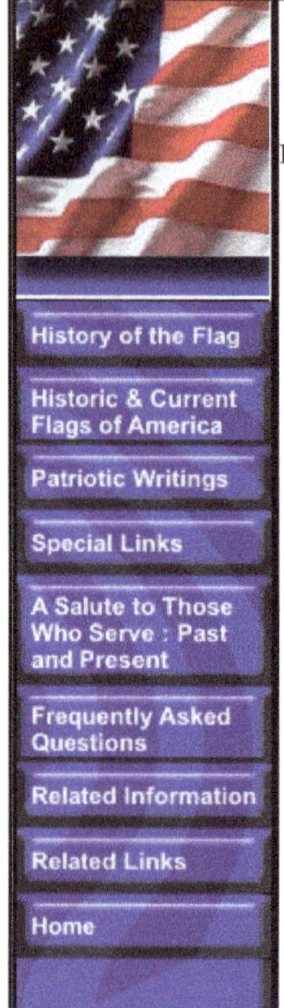

Navigation (left sidebar):

- History of the Flag
- Historic & Current Flags of America
- Patriotic Writings
- Special Links
- A Salute to Those Who Serve : Past and Present
- Frequently Asked Questions
- Related Information
- Related Links
- Home

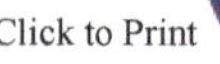

Site Key: Click to Listen Click to Print *Search:* | GO |

The Service Flag of the United States

The Service Flag is available for purchase from my friends at U.S. Flag Depot, Inc.

The graphic above showing the Service Flag is borrowed from
the National Archives Online Exhibit Hall about the Poster Art of World War II.
The Service Flag History below is from the U.S. Naval Academy

The History of the Service Flag

The Service Flag is an official banner authorized by the Department of Defense for display by families who have members serving in the Armed Forces during any period of war or hostilities the United States may be engaged in for the duration of such hostilities.

The history of the Service Flag is as patriotic and touching as the symbolism each star represents to the families that display them.

The service flag (also known as "blue star banners" or "son in service flags") was designed and patented by World War I Army Captain Robert L. Queissner of the 5th Ohio Infantry who had two sons serving on the front line. The flag quickly became the unofficial symbol of a child in service. President Wilson became part of its history when in 1918 he approved a suggestion made by the Women's Committee of the Council of National Defenses that mothers who had lost a child serving in the war to wear a gold gilt star on the traditional black mourning arm band.

This led to the tradition to cover the blue star with a gold star on the Service flag to indicate that the service member has died or been killed.

The color of the stars is also symbolic in that the blue star represents hope and pride and the gold star represents sacrifice to the cause of liberty and freedom.

During World War II, the practice of displaying the service flag became much more widespread. In 1942, the Blue Star Mothers of America was founded as a veteran service organization and was part of a movement to provide care packages to military members serving overseas and also provide assistance to families who encountered hardships as a result of their son or husband serving during the war.

Virtually every home and organization displayed banners to indicate the number of members of the family or organization serving in the Armed Forces, and again, covered those blue stars with a gold star to represent each member that died.

In 1960, Congress chartered the Blue Star Mothers of America as a veterans service organization and in 1966, the Department of Defense revised the specifications for the design, manufacture and display of the Service Flag.

The Department of Defense specifies that family members authorized to display the flag include the wife, husband, mother, father, stepfather, parent through adoption, foster parents who stand or stood in loco parentis, children, stepchildren, children through adoption, brothers, sisters, half brothers and half sisters of a member of the Armed Forces of the United States. The flag should be displayed in a window of the residence of person who are members of the immediate family.

The Service Flag may also be displayed by an organization to honor the members of that organization serving in the Armed Forces during a period of war or hostilities.

How to Display the Service Flag

The Service Flag is an indoor flag and should be flown facing out from the front window of the home or organization.

If the U.S. flag is also displayed with the Service Flag, the U.S. flag should be of equal or greater proportions and should take the place of honor above the Service Flag.

If a gold star is added to the Service Flag, it should take the position of honor and be placed over the blue star that is positioned closest to the staff.

The gold star should be smaller than the blue star to create a blue border surrounding the gold star.

This page is maintained by Duane Streufert, Contact Us.
Questions or comments welcome!
This Site Established on 20 November 1994.
Last Updated 10 February 2005.
Web Design and Development by Visionary Enterprises

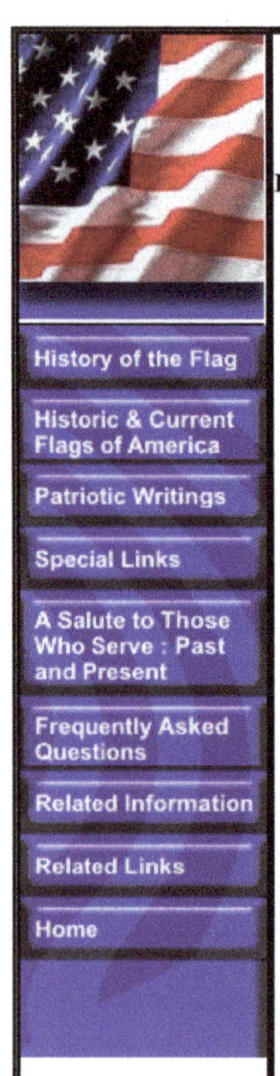

Site Key: 🔊 Click to Listen 🖨 Click to Print　*Search:* [　　　　] GO

- History of the Flag
- Historic & Current Flags of America
- Patriotic Writings
- Special Links
- A Salute to Those Who Serve : Past and Present
- Frequently Asked Questions
- Related Information
- Related Links
- Home

Washington's Flag 1775

Washington's Flag 1775: This was the personal flag of the Commander-In-Chief during the Revolutionary War. A reproduction of this flag flies today at Washington's Headquarters, Valley Forge.

Official Flags of the United States				
13-Star	15-Star	20-Star	21-Star	23-Star
24-Star	25-Star	26-Star	27-Star	28-Star
29-Star	30-Star	31-Star	32-Star	33-Star
34-Star	35-Star	36-Star	37-Star	38-Star
43-Star	44-Star	45-Star	46-Star	48-Star
	49-Star		50-Star	

This page is maintained by Duane Streufert, Contact Us.
Questions or comments welcome!
This Site Established on 20 November 1994.
Last Updated 10 February 2005.
Web Design and Development by Visionary Enterprises

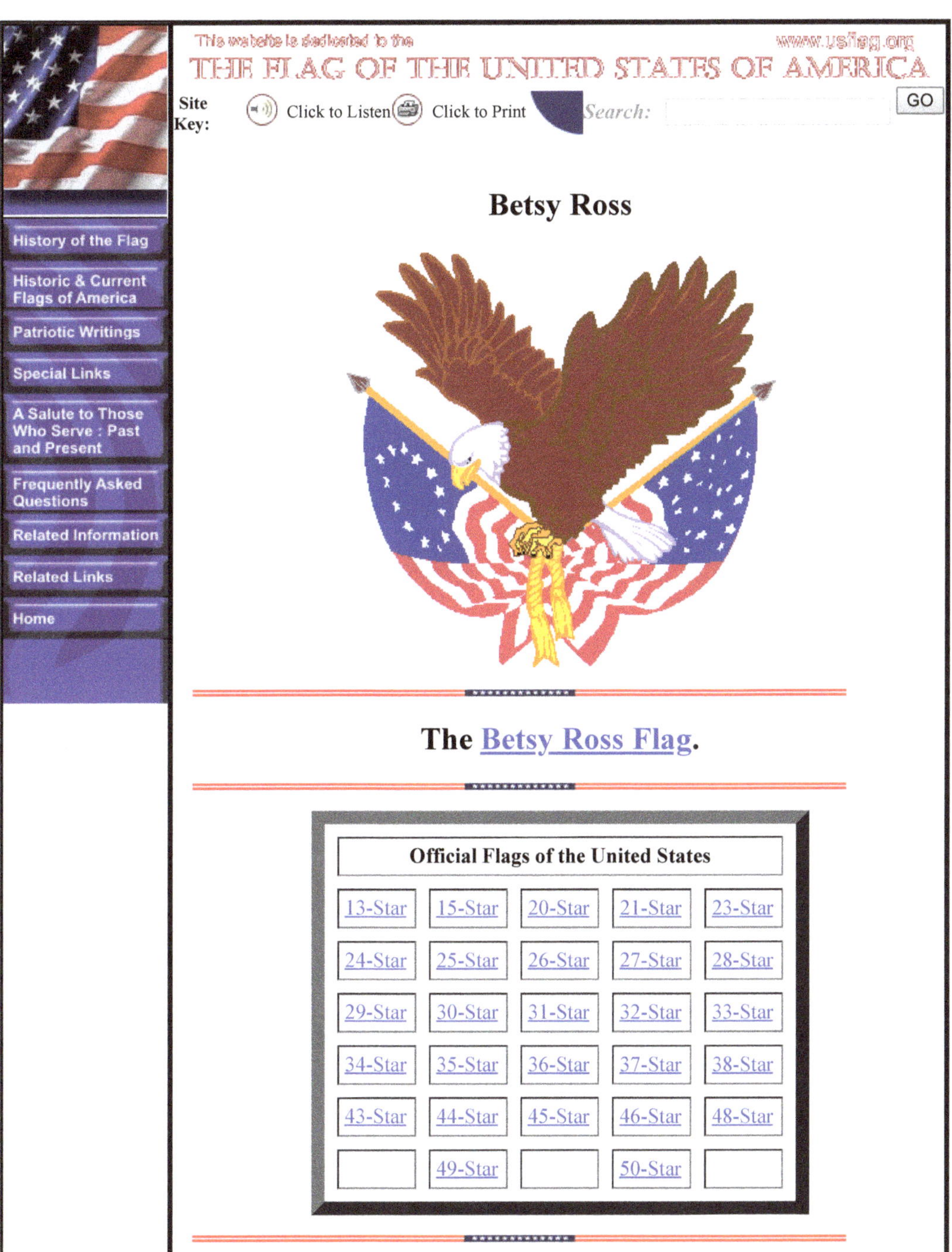

Betsy Ross

The [Betsy Ross Flag](#).

Official Flags of the United States

13-Star	15-Star	20-Star	21-Star	23-Star
24-Star	25-Star	26-Star	27-Star	28-Star
29-Star	30-Star	31-Star	32-Star	33-Star
34-Star	35-Star	36-Star	37-Star	38-Star
43-Star	44-Star	45-Star	46-Star	48-Star
	49-Star		50-Star	

Navigation menu:

- History of the Flag
- Historic & Current Flags of America
- Patriotic Writings
- Special Links
- A Salute to Those Who Serve : Past and Present
- Frequently Asked Questions
- Related Information
- Related Links
- Home

The State Flags in the table below are available for purchase from my friends at [U.S. Flag Depot, Inc.](#)

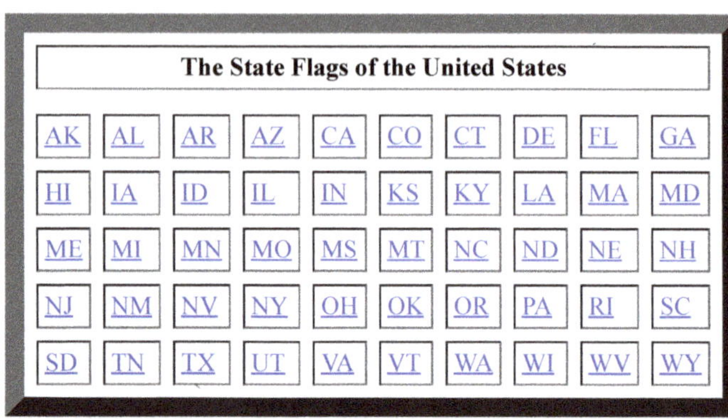

The [Presidents](#) Flag.
The [Service Flag](#) was well known during World War II.

These are some Flags used during the Revolutionary and Civil Wars;

- [Washington's Flag 1775](#)
- Flags with a [Snake motif](#), "Don't Tread On Me", The Gadsden Flag and the Culpeper Flag.
- [Grand Union 1775](#)
- [The Bennington Flag](#)
- [The Serapis Flag](#)
- [The Guilford Flag](#)
- The [Flags of the Confederate States of America](#), 1861-1865.

This page is maintained by Duane Streufert, [Contact Us](#).
Questions or comments welcome!
This Site Established on 20 November 1994.
Last Updated 10 February 2005.
Web Design and Development by [Visionary Enterprises](#)

Site Key: Click to Listen   Click to Print   *Search:*   GO

The original Pledge of Allegiance

"I pledge allegiance to my Flag and the Republic for which it stands-one nation indivisible-with liberty and justice for all."

On September 8,1892, the Boston based "The Youth's Companion" magazine published a few words for students to repeat on Columbus Day that year. Written by Francis Bellamy,the circulation manager and native of Rome, New York, and reprinted on thousands of leaflets, was sent out to public schools across the country. On October 12, 1892, the quadricentennial of Columbus' arrival, more than 12 million children recited the Pledge of Allegiance, thus beginning a required school-day ritual.

At the first National Flag Conference in Washington D.C., on June14, 1923, a change was made. For clarity, the words "the Flag of the United States" replaced "my flag". In the following years various other changes were suggested but were never formally adopted.

It was not until 1942 that Congress officially recognized the Pledge of Allegiance. One year later, in June 1943, the Supreme Court ruled that school children could not be forced to recite it. In fact,today only half of our fifty states have laws that encourage the recitation of the Pledge of Allegiance in the classroom!

In June of 1954 an amendment was made to add the words "under God". Then-President Dwight D. Eisenhower said "In this way we are reaffirming the transcendence of religious faith in America's heritage and future; in this way we shall constantly strengthen those spiritual weapons which forever will be our country's most powerful resource in peace and war."

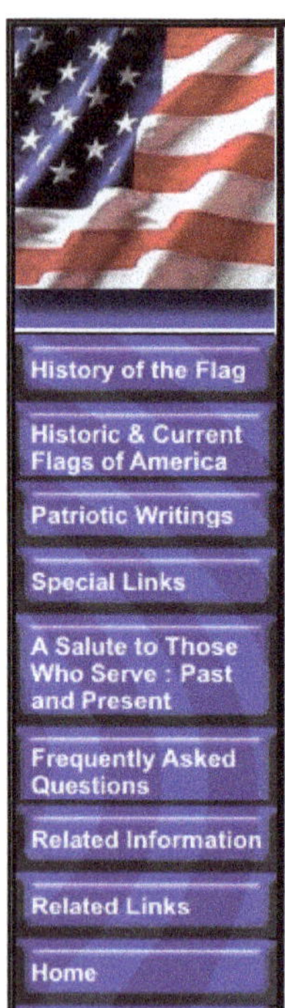

History of the Flag

Historic & Current Flags of America

Patriotic Writings

Special Links

A Salute to Those Who Serve : Past and Present

Frequently Asked Questions

Related Information

Related Links

Home

This website is dedicated to the

THE FLAG OF THE UNITED STATES OF AMERICA

www.usflag.org

Site Key:

 Click to Listen Click to Print *Search:* GO

Evolution of the United States Flag

No one knows with **absolute certainty** who designed the first stars and stripes or who made it. Congressman Francis Hopkinson seems most likely to have designed it, and few historians believe that Betsy Ross, a Philadelphia seamstress, made the first one.

Until the Executive Order of June 24, 1912, neither the order of the stars nor the proportions of the flag was prescribed. Consequently, flags dating before this period sometimes show unusual arrangements of the stars and odd proportions, these features being left to the discretion of the flag maker. In general, however, straight rows of stars and proportions similar to those later adopted officially were used. The principal acts affecting the flag of the United States are the following:

- On June 14, 1777, in order to establish an official flag for the new nation, the Continental Congress passed the **first Flag Act**: "Resolved, That the flag of the United States be made of thirteen stripes, alternate red and white; that the union be thirteen stars, white in a blue field, representing a new Constellation."
- Act of January 13, 1794 - provided for 15 stripes and 15 stars after May 1795.
- Act of April 4, 1818 - provided for 13 stripes and one star for each state, to be added to the flag on the 4th of July following the admission of each new state, signed by President Monroe.
- Executive Order of President Taft dated June 24, 1912 - established proportions of the flag and provided for arrangement of the stars in six horizontal rows of eight each, a single point of each star to be upward.
- Executive Order of President Eisenhower dated January 3, 1959 - provided for the arrangement of the stars in seven rows of seven stars each, staggered horizontally and vertically.
- Executive Order of President Eisenhower dated August 21, 1959 - provided for the arrangement of the stars in nine rows of stars staggered horizon tally and eleven rows of stars staggered vertically.

This page is maintained by Duane Streufert, Contact Us.
Questions or comments welcome!
This Site Established on 20 November 1994.
Last Updated 10 February 2005.
Web Design and Development by Visionary Enterprises

I am the Flag

by Ruth Apperson Rous

I am the flag of the United States of America.

I was born on June 14, 1777, in Philadelphia.

There the Continental Congress adopted my stars and stripes as the national flag.

My thirteen stripes alternating red and white, with a union of thirteen white stars in a field of blue, represented a new constellation, a new nation dedicated to the personal and religious liberty of mankind.

Today fifty stars signal from my union, one for each of the fifty sovereign states in the greatest constitutional republic the world has ever known.

My colors symbolize the patriotic ideals and spiritual qualities of the citizens of my country.

My red stripes proclaim the fearless courage and integrity of American men and boys and the self-sacrifice and devotion of American mothers and daughters.

My white stripes stand for liberty and equality for all.

My blue is the blue of heaven, loyalty, and faith.

I represent these eternal principles: liberty, justice, and humanity.

I embody American freedom: freedom of speech, religion, assembly, the press, and the sanctity of the home.

I typify that indomitable spirit of determination brought to my land by Christopher Columbus and by all my forefathers - the Pilgrims, Puritans, settlers at James town and Plymouth.

I am as old as my nation.

I am a living symbol of my nation's law: the Constitution of the United States and the Bill of Rights.

I voice Abraham Lincoln's philosophy: "A government of the people, by the people,for the people."

I stand guard over my nation's schools, the seedbed of good citizenship and true patriotism.

I am displayed in every schoolroom throughout my nation; every schoolyard has a flag pole for my display.

Daily thousands upon thousands of boys and girls pledge their allegiance to me and my country.

I have my own law—Public Law 829, "The Flag Code" - which definitely states my correct use and display for all occasions and situations.

I have my special day, Flag Day. June 14 is set aside to honor my birth.

Americans, I am the sacred emblem of your country. I symbolize your birthright, your heritage of liberty purchased with blood and sorrow.

I am your title deed of freedom, which is yours to enjoy and hold in trust for posterity.

If you fail to keep this sacred trust inviolate, if I am nullified and destroyed, you and your children will become slaves to dictators and despots.

Eternal vigilance is your price of freedom.

As you see me silhouetted against the peaceful skies of my country, remind yourself that I am the flag of your country, that I stand for what you are - no more, no less.

Guard me well, lest your freedom perish from the earth.

Dedicate your lives to those principles for which I stand: "One nation under God, indivisible, with liberty and justice for all."

I was created in freedom. I made my first appearance in a battle for human liberty.

God grant that I may spend eternity in my "land of the free and the home of the brave" and that I shall ever be known as "Old Glory," the flag of the United States of America.

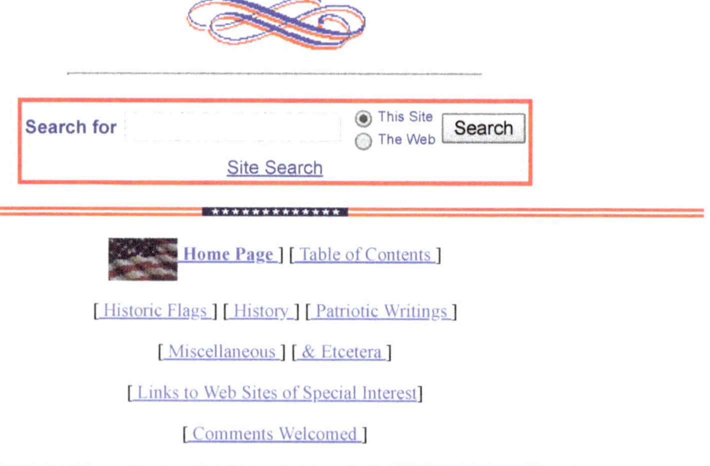

[Home Page] [Table of Contents]

[Historic Flags] [History] [Patriotic Writings]

[Miscellaneous] [& Etcetera]

[Links to Web Sites of Special Interest]

[Comments Welcomed]

Betsy Ross and the American Flag

Frequently Asked Questions

Who created the U.S. flag? Was it Betsy Ross?

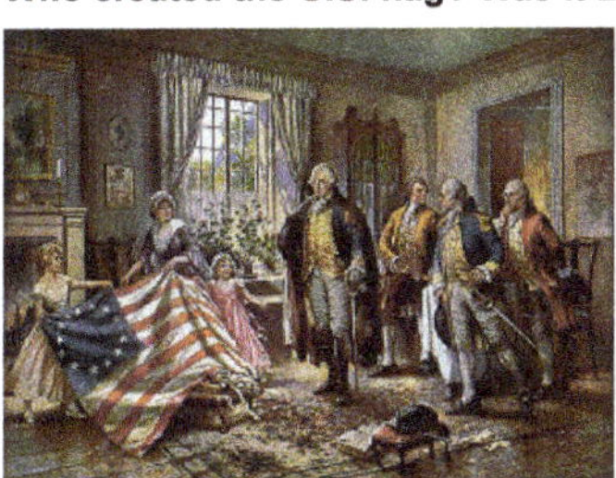

(images/rossbetsy.jpg)

The Birth of Old Glory
Percy Moran, 1917
LOC id: cph.3g02791 (http://www.loc.gov/pictures/resource/cph.3g02791/)

Maybe! The evidence is compelling, though not conclusive. Several of her relatives testified to having heard extensive details of the flag's creation. The testimony is entirely plausible, and no other claimant has ever produced any equally compelling evidence, but no preserved documents from the Continental Congress or the personal correspondance of George Washington or any related figures has emerged to either confirm or contradict the claims made by Betsy's decendents.

While the evidence is simply not sufficient to definitively classsify it as a fact or a fiction, you can examine that evidence yourself and draw your own conclusions. You can read the testimony of William Canby (more/canby.htm) and the affidavits of Rachel Fletcher (flagaffs.html), Sophia Hildebrant (flagaffs2.html) and Margaret Boggs (flagaffs3.html)

Are these people telling the truth? Is it all a carefully orchestrated hoax? Somewhere in between? That's up to *you* . . .

Why do some people think that Betsy Ross's creation of the flag is a myth?

Betsy's creation of the flag is not an established historical fact, like the signing of the Declaration of Independence (../declaration/) in Independence Hall (../tour/independence-hall.htm) in Philadelphia, or Washington's winter at Valley Forge (../valleyforge/). Those events quite definitely took place, and were public knowledge from the beginning.

Most of us learned about all those things in school. Upon learning later that Betsy Ross's flag creation has not been established with the same level of certainty as those other events, some conclude that it was therefore a myth or a hoax, like George Washington and the cherry tree. That's a genuine American myth. Betsy is not.

The available evidence is insufficient to establish Betsy as the creator of the flag with certaintly. But it's entirely plausible and consistent with the evidence we do have. Some suggest that sexism explains the reluctance to accept Betsy's achievements, but perhaps it is simply a misunderstanding of the process of history. Historians don't have all the answers. They don't have a complete and reliable record of the past. Historians need to interpret the available evidence to construct as accurate a picture of the past as they can, and sometimes the available evidence is incomplete and inconclusive. That's very different from a hoax or a myth.

(//www.netseer.com/netseer-inimage-ads/?utm_source=info_button&utm_med

What do the red, white, and blue of the flag repres

The Continental Congress left no record to show why it chose the colors. However, in 1782, the Congress of the Confederation chose these same colors for the Great Seal of the United States and listed their meaning as follows:

- Red: Valor and hardiness,
- White: Purity and innocence
- Blue: Vigilance, perseverance, and justice.

According to legend, George Washington interpreted the elements of the flag this way: the stars were taken from the sky, the red from the British colors, and the white stripes signified the secession from the home country. However, there is no official designation or meaning for the colors of the flag.

Why are the stars in a circle?

The stars were in a circle so that no one colony would be viewed above another. It is reported that George Washington said, "Let the 13 stars in a circle stand as a new constellation in the heavens."

If Betsy sewed the flag, who designed it?

In an affidavit made public in 1870, Betsy Ross's daughter, Rachel Fletcher, testified (flagaffs.html) :

> "[The committee] showed her [Betsy Ross] a drawing roughly executed, of the flag as it was proposed to be made by the committee, and that she saw in it some defects in its proportions and the arrangement and shape of the stars. That she said it was square and a flag should be one third longer than its width, that the stars were scattered promiscuously over the field, and she said they should be either in lines or in some adopted form as a circle, or a star, and that the stars were six-pointed in the drawing, and she said they should be five pointed."

(http://www.ushistory.org/store/betsy.asp)

Why would Betsy Ross be chosen to make the flag?

It was usual in that day for upholsterers to be flagmakers. As Betsy Ross prayed in the pew next to George Washington and had already sewn buttons for him, and she was a niece of George Ross, it is not exceptional that these members of the Flag Committee formed by the Continental Congress would call upon Betsy Ross to make the flag.

Was this her house?

It is known that Betsy Ross rented rooms here. At the time of the alleged flag creation, she was either here at 239 Arch Street or next door at 241 Arch, where the garden is now. House numbers on her street between the years 1785 and 1857 were registered using three different numbering systems, making the determination very tricky. If you are interested in historical detective work, you'll enjoy the methodical, historical approach used by experts: check out the Was this her house? (prove239.html) page.

Where is the first flag?

(//www.netseer.com/netseer-inimage-ads/?utm_source=info_button&utm_me

We have very little definitive information about the first flag. Betsy's association with the flag arose through an oral history brought to public attention long after the flag's creation. No actual flag exists that is alleged to have been the first flag created by Betsy Ross.

Why is the flag called "Old Glory"?

In 1831, Captain William Driver, a shipmaster from Salem, Massachusetts, left on one of his many world voyages. Friends presented him with a flag of 24 stars. As the banner opened to the ocean breeze, he exclaimed, "Old Glory." He kept his flag for many years, protecting it during the Civil War, until it was flown over the Tennessee capital. His "Old Glory" became a nickname for all American flags.

Who was Mary Pickersgill?

Mary Young Pickersgill sewed the very large (30'x42') Star-Spangled Banner in the summer of 1813. It flew over Fort McHenry during the War of 1812 (1812-1814) and was the inspiration for Francis Scott Key to write what would become our National Anthem. Pickersgill's flag today hangs at the Smithsonian Institution in Washington, DC. Her house still stands as a museum you can visit in Baltimore, Maryland.

What is a vexillologist?

A vexillologist is an expert on flags and ensigns. A vexillum (plural vexilla) is a military standard or flag used by ancient Roman troops.

Many people discover among their family relics a certificate from the American Flag House and Betsy Ross Memorial Association. What is it?

(images/flaghouse.jpg)

Over two million of these certificates were sold starting in 1898 in order to raise funds needed to preserve the Betsy Ross House. These certificates were receipts or "thank-yous" for contributions of 10 cents. The Association went out of business in 1935. The only "value" to these is the knowledge that the recipient participated in the preservation of the Betsy Ross House.

Help Support USHistory.org! Buy a flag or poster!
(http://store.ushistory.org/showcat.asp?cid=27)

USHistory.org (http://ushistory.org)
(https://www.facebook.com/independencehallassociation)

Betsy Ross

Elizabeth Griscom Ross (1752-1836), was a Philadelphia seamstress, married to John Ross, an upholsterer who was killed in a munitions explosion in 1776. She kept the upholstery shop going and lived on Arch Street, not too far from the State House on Chestnut, where history was being made almost every day. According to most historians, she has been incorrectly credited with designing the first Stars and Stripes. The story has enormous popularity, yet the facts do not substantiate it. Lets begin with the legend itself.

George Washington was a frequent visitor to the home of Mrs. Ross before receiving command of the army. She embroidered his shirt ruffles and did many other things for him. He knew her skill with a needle. Now the General of the Continental Army, George Washington appeared on Mrs. Ross's dooorstep around the first of June, 1776, with two representatives of Congress, Colonel Ross and Robert Morris. They asked that she make a flag according to a rough drawing they carried with them. At Mrs.Ross's suggestion, Washington redrew the flag design in pencil in her back parlor to employ stars of five points instead of six. ("Her version" of the flag for the new republic was not used until six years later.)

This account of the creation of our first flag was first brought to light in 1870 by one of her grandsons, William J. Canby, at a meeting of the Historical Society of Pennsylvania. This took place **94 years** after the event supposedly took place! Mr. Canby was a boy of eleven years when Mrs. Ross died in his home.

In the many years since the story was told, numerous historians have conducted vigorous searches into extant government records, personal diaries,and writings of Washington and his contemporaries and none of them have been able to verify the claims of Canby. One verifiable fact is this; the minutes of the State Navy Board of Pennsylvania for May 29, 1777, say in part "An order on William Webb to Elizabeth Ross for fourteen pounds twelve shillings, and two pence, for making ship's colours,&c, put into Richards store". The minutes show that Elizabeth Ross made ship's colors for Pennsylvania state ships. Some of the facts, among others, that have been discovered by this research that cast doubt on Canby's claim are these; He asserted that the stars and stripes were in common if not general use soon after the signing of the Declaration of Independence, nearly a year **before** the resolution of Congress proclaiming the flag. There is **no** record of the flag being discussed or of a committee being appointed for the design of the flag in either the Journals of the Continental Congress or the diaries and writings of Washington around this time. Meetings with Colonel Ross and Robert Morris cannot be documented. Further, it is illogical to assume that Washington was present at the alleged meeting with Betsy Ross on the design of the flag when it is known that he wanted a national standard made for the use of the army in 1779.

But I think that the question that begs to be asked is; Why have so many generations of Americans come to accept this legend as fact? After Canby's death, a book written by his brother George Canby and nephew Lloyd Balderson was published in 1909. The book, The Evolution of the American Flag, presented in more detail the claims for Betsy Ross made by William Canby in 1870. Among other things, the authors describe the formation of the Betsy Ross Memorial Association, and reproduced a painting by Charles H. Weisgerber depicting the alleged meeting of the committee of Congress with Betsy Ross. The picture, entitled Birth of Our Nations Flag, is actually a composite portrait made up of from pictures of her granddaughters and other decendants. The artist took liberties with history by painting the stars in the flag in a circle. This painting, incidently, stirred a great deal of public interest in the subject when it was first exibited, at the Columbian Exposition in Chicago in 1893. Following this, money to purchase the Betsy Ross house in Philadelphia was raised by selling ten-cent subscriptions to the American Flag House and Betsy Ross Memorial Association, incorporated in 1898. Each contributor received a certificate of membership that included a picture of the house, her grave in Mt. Moriah Cemetery in Philadelphia, and a color reproduction of the Weisberger painting. This campaign gave the legend wide publicity and the Weisberger painting was reproduced in school history textbooks thoughout the United States!

In the days of Betsy Ross we did not have the benefit of a frenetic press corps to witness, probe, and record the events of the day. Careful historians do not accept the legend and neither should we. At the same time, there often seems to be a wistful regret, best expressed, perhaps, by President Woodrow Wilson when asked his opinion of the story. He replied, **"Would that it were true!"**

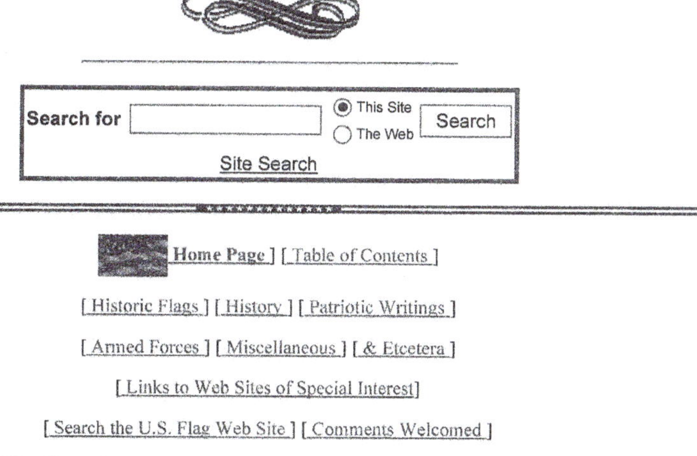

v

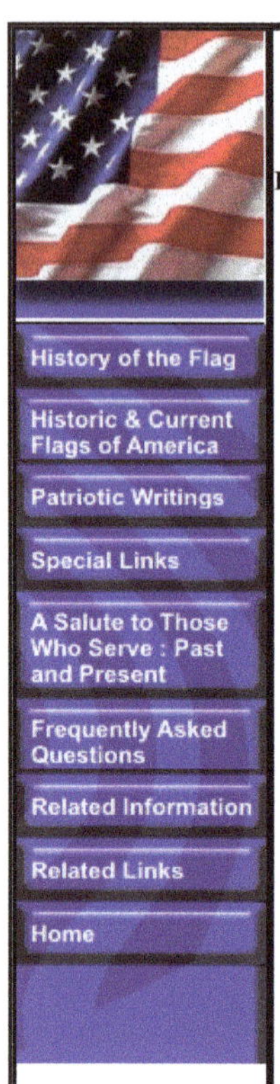

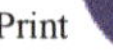

Site Key: Click to Listen Click to Print *Search:* | GO |

- History of the Flag
- Historic & Current Flags of America
- Patriotic Writings
- Special Links
- A Salute to Those Who Serve : Past and Present
- Frequently Asked Questions
- Related Information
- Related Links
- Home

"OLD GLORY!"

This famous name was coined by Captain William Driver, a shipmaster of Salem, Massachusetts, in 1831. As he was leaving on one of his many voyages aboard the brig CHARLES DOGGETT - and this one would climax with the rescue of the mutineers of the **BOUNTY** - some friends presented him with a beautiful flag of twenty four stars. As the banner opened to the ocean breeze for the first time, he exclaimed "Old Glory!"

He retired to Nashville in 1837, taking his treasured flag from his sea days with him. By the time the Civil War erupted, most everyone in and around Nashville recognized Captain Driver's "Old Glory." When Tennesee seceded from the Union, Rebels were determined to destroy his flag, but repeated searches revealed no trace of the hated banner.

Then on February 25th, 1862, Union forces captured Nashville and raised the American flag over the capital. It was a rather small ensign and immediately folks began asking Captain Driver if "Old Glory" still existed. Happy to have soldiers with him this time, Captain Driver went home and began ripping at the seams of his bedcover. As the stitches holding the quilt-top to the batting unraveled, the onlookers peered inside and saw the 24-starred original "Old Glory"!

Captain Driver gently gathered up the flag and returned with the soldiers to the capitol. Though he was sixty years old, the Captain climbed up to the tower to replace the smaller banner with his beloved flag. The Sixth Ohio Regiment cheered and saluted - and later adopted the nickname "Old Glory" as their own, telling and re-telling the story of Captain Driver's devotion to the flag we honor yet today.

Captain Driver's grave is located in the old Nashville City Cemetery, and is one of three (3) places authorized by act of Congress where the Flag of the United States may be flown 24 hours a day.

A caption above a faded black and white picture in the book, The Stars and the Stripes, states that " 'Old Glory' may no longer be opened to be photographed, and no color photograph is available." Visible in the photo in the lower right corner of the canton is an appliqued anchor, Captain Driver's very personal note. "Old Glory" is the most illustrious of a number of flags - both Northern and Confederate - reputed to have been similarly hidden, then later revealed as times changed. The flag was given to his granddaughter or neice and she later donated it to the Smithsonian.

This page is maintained by Duane Streufert, Contact Us.
Questions or comments welcome!
This Site Established on 20 November 1994.
Last Updated 10 February 2005.
Web Design and Development by Visionary Enterprises

The First United States Flag

The 13 Star Flag is available for purchase from my friends at U.S. Flag Depot, Inc.

The First Official United States Flag: This 13-Star Flag became the Official United States Flag on June14th, 1777 and is the result of the congressional action that took place on that date. Much evidence exists pointing to Congressman Francis Hopkinson as the person responsible for its design.The only President to serve under this flag was George Washington (1789-1797). This Flag was to last for a period of 18 years.

Each star *and* stripe represented a Colony of which there were thirteen, united nearly one year earlier by the Declaration of Independence. The thirteen Colonies are listed below with the date that each ratified the Constitution and became a State.

- (1st) Delaware December 7th, 1787
- (2nd) Pennsylvania December 12th,1787
- (3rd) New Jersey December18th, 1787
- (4th) Georgia January 2nd, 1788
- (5th) Connecticut January 9th, 1788
- (6th) Massachusetts February 6th, 1788
- (7th) Maryland April 28th, 1788
- (8th) South Carolina May 23rd, 1788
- (9th) New Hampshire June 21st, 1788
- (10th) Virginia June 25th, 1788
- (11th) New York July 25th, 1788
- (12th) North Carolina November 21st, 1789
- (13th) Rhode Island May 29th, 1790

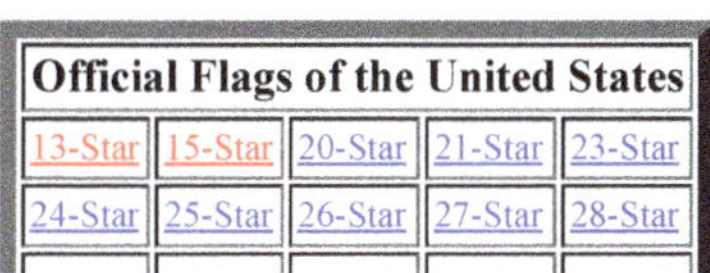

Official Flags of the United States				
13-Star	15-Star	20-Star	21-Star	23-Star
24-Star	25-Star	26-Star	27-Star	28-Star

29-Star	30-Star	31-Star	32-Star	33-Star
34-Star	35-Star	36-Star	37-Star	38-Star
43-Star	44-Star	45-Star	46-Star	48-Star
	49-Star		50-Star	

Search for [___________] ◉ This Site ○ The Web [**Search**]

Site Search

★★★★★★★★★★★★★

[**Home Page**] [Table of Contents]

[Historic Flags] [History] [Patriotic Writings]

[Miscellaneous] [& Etcetera]

[Links to Web Sites of Special Interest]

[Comments Welcomed]

★★★★★★★★★★★★★

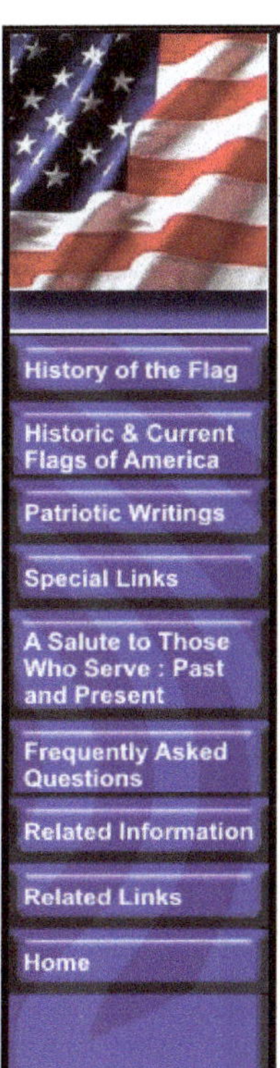

History of the Flag

Historic & Current Flags of America

Patriotic Writings

Special Links

A Salute to Those Who Serve : Past and Present

Frequently Asked Questions

Related Information

Related Links

Home

This website is dedicated to the

www.usflag.org

THE FLAG OF THE UNITED STATES OF AMERICA

Site Key:  Click to Listen  Click to Print   *Search:* [GO]

Francis Scott Key

1780-1843

Francis Scott Key was a respected young lawyer living in Georgetown just west of where the modern day Key Bridge crosses the Potomac River (the house was torn down after years of neglect in 1947). He made his home there from 1804 to around 1833 with his wife Mary and their six sons and five daughters. At the time, Georgetown was a thriving town of 5,000 people just a few miles from the Capitol, the White House, and the Federal buildings of Washington.

But, after war broke out in 1812 over Britian's attempts to regulate American shipping and other activities while Britain was at war with France, all was not tranquil in Georgetown. The British had entered Chesapeake Bay on August 19th, 1814, and by the evening of the 24th of August, the British had invaded and captured Washington. They set fire to the Capitol and the White House, the flames visible 40 miles away in Baltimore.

President James Madison,his wife Dolley, and his Cabinet had already fled to a safer location. Such was their haste to leave that they had had to rip the Stuart portrait of George Washington from the walls without its frame!

A thunderstorm at dawn kept the fires from spreading. The next day more buildings were burned and again a thunderstorm dampened the fires. Having done their work the British troops returned to their ships in and around the Chesapeake Bay.

In the days following the attack on Washington, the American forces prepared for the assault on Baltimore (population 40,000) that they knew would come by both land and sea. Word soon reached Francis Scott Key that the British had carried off an elderly and much loved town physician of Upper Marlboro, Dr. William Beanes, and was being held on the British flagship TONNANT. The townsfolk feared that Dr. Beanes would be hanged. They asked Francis Scott Key for his help, and he agreed, and arranged to have Col. John Skinner, an American agent for prisoner exchange to accompany him.

On the morning of September 3rd, he and Col. Skinner set sail from Baltimore aboard a sloop flying a flag of truce approved by President Madison. On the 7th they found and boarded the TONNANT to confer with Gen. Ross and Adm. Alexander Cochrane. At first they refused to release Dr. Beanes. But Key and Skinner produced a pouch of letters written by wounded British prisoners praising the care they were receiving from the Americans, among them Dr. Beanes. The British officers relented but would not release the three Americans immediately because they had seen and heard too much of the preparations for the attack on Baltimore. They were placed under guard, first aboard the H.M.S. Surprise, then onto the sloop and forced to wait out the battle behind the British fleet.

Now let's go back to the summer of 1813 for a moment. At the star-shaped Fort McHenry, the commander, Maj. George Armistead, asked for a flag so big that "the British would have no trouble seeing it from a distance". Two officers, a Commodore and a General, were sent to the Baltimore home of Mary Young Pickersgill, a "maker of colours," and commisioned the flag. Mary and her thirteen year old daughter Caroline, working in an upstairs front bedroom, used 400 yards of best quality wool bunting. They cut 15 stars that measured two feet from point to point. Eight red and seven white stripes, each two feet wide, were cut. Laying out the material on the malthouse floor of Claggett's Brewery, a neighborhood establishment, the flag was sewn together. By August it was finished. It measured 30 by 42 feet and cost $405.90. The Baltimore Flag House, a museum, now occupies her premises, which were restored in 1953.

At 7 a.m. on the morning of September 13, 1814, the British bombardment began, and the flag was ready to meet the enemy. The bombardment continued for 25 hours,the British firing 1,500 bombshells that weighed as much as 220 pounds and carried lighted fuses that would supposedly cause it to explode when it reached its target. But they weren't very dependable and often blew up in mid air. From special small boats the British fired the new Congreve rockets that traced wobbly arcs of red flame across the sky. The Americans had sunk 22 vessels so a close approach by the British was not possible. That evening the connonading stopped, but at about 1 a.m. on the 14th, the British fleet roared to life, lighting the rainy night sky with grotesque fireworks.

Key, Col. Skinner, and Dr. Beanes watched the battle with apprehension. They knew that as long as the shelling continued, Fort McHenry had not surrendered. But, long before daylight there came a sudden and mysterious silence. What the three Americans did not know was that the British land assault on Baltimore as well as the naval attack, had been abandoned. Judging Baltimore as being too costly a prize, the British officers ordered a retreat.

Waiting in the predawn darkness, Key waited for the sight that would end his anxiety; the joyous sight of Gen. Armisteads great flag blowing in the breeze. When at last daylight came, **the flag was still there!**

Being an amatuer poet and having been so uniquely inspired, Key began to write on the back of a letter he had in his pocket. Sailing back to Baltimore he composed more lines and in his lodgings at the Indian Queen Hotel he finished the poem. Judge J. H. Nicholson, his brother-in-law, took it to a printer and copies were circulated around Baltimore under the title "Defence of Fort M'Henry". Two of these copies survive. It was printed in a newspaper for the first time in the Baltimore Patriot on September 20th,1814, then in papers as far away as Georgia and New Hampshire. To the verses was added a note "Tune: Anacreon in Heaven." In October a Baltimore actor sang Key's new song in a public performance and called it "The Star-Spangled Banner".

Immediately popular, it remained just one of several patriotic airs until it was finally adopted as our national anthem on March 3, 1931. But the actual words were not included in the legal documents. Key himself had written several versions with slight variations so discrepancies in the exact wording still occur.

The flag, our beloved Star-Spangled Banner, went on view ,for the first time after flying over Fort McHenry, on January 1st,1876 at the Old State House in Philadelphia for the nations' Centennial celebration. It now resides in the Smithsonian Institution's

Museum of American History. An opaque curtain shields the now fragile flag from light and dust. The flag is exposed for viewing for a few moments once every hour during museum hours.

Francis Scott Key was a witness to the last enemy fire to fall on Fort McHenry. The Fort was designed by a Frenchman named Jean Foncin and was named for then Secretary of war James McHenry. Fort McHenry holds the unique designation of national monument and historic shrine.

Since May 30th, 1949 the flag has **flown continuously**, by a Joint Resolution of Congress, over the monument marking the site of Francis Scott Key's birthplace, Terra Rubra Farm, Carroll County, Keymar, Maryland.

The copy that Key wrote in his hotel September 14,1814, remained in the Nicholson family for 93 years. In 1907 it was sold to Henry Walters of Baltimore. In 1934 it was bought at auction in New York from the Walters estate by the Walters Art Gallery, Baltimore for $26,400. The Walters Gallery in 1953 sold the manuscript to the Maryland Historical Society for the same price. Another copy that Key made is in the Library of Congress.

Related Site: The Patriots of Fort McHenry

This page is maintained by Duane Streufert, Contact Us.
Questions or comments welcome!
This Site Established on 20 November 1994.
Last Updated 10 February 2005.
Web Design and Development by Visionary Enterprises

The Star Spangled Banner, the 15 Star Flag

The 15 Star Flag is available for purchase from my friends at U.S. Flag Depot, Inc.

The Star Spangled Banner: This Flag became the Official United States Flag on May 1st,1795. Two stars were added for the admission of Vermont (the 14th State on March 4th, 1791) and Kentucky (the 15th State on June 1st, 1792, and was to last for 23 years. The five Presidents who served under this flag were; George Washington (1789-1797), John Adams (1797-1801), Thomas Jefferson (1801-1809), James Madison (1809-1817), and James Monroe (1817-1825).

The 15-star, **15-stripe** flag was authorized by the Flag Act of January 13, 1794, adding 2 stripes and 2 Stars. The regulation went into effect on May 1, 1795. This flag was the only U.S. Flag to have more than 13 stripes. It was immortalized by Francis Scott Key during the bombardment of Fort McHenry, Sept 13, 1814. The image above is representative of the actual flag that flew over Fort McHenry on that day and which is now preserved in the Smithsonian Museum. You can notice the "tilt" in some of the stars just as in the original Star Spangled Banner.

Where the original Star Spangled Banner went...

1814

The battle occurred, and the flag won its glory. Armistead was promoted to Lt. Colonel by Madison. Armistead died in service on April 25, 1818. He acquired the flag sometime before that date, but at this point it is unknown how.

1818

Armistead died and "legend" says that the flag was used in his funeral. However, in all of the newspaper accounts of Armistead's funeral, there is no mention of the flag being displayed at it. At his death the flag passed to his widow, Louisa Armistead.

1824

The flag was used in a reception for General Lafayette.

. 1861

Louisa Armistead died on October 3, 1861, and in her will left the flag to her daughter, Georgiana Armistead Appleton. The flag was sent to England for safe keeping during the Civil War, according to one of the Armistead family members, who made this statement in a newspaper interview in the 1880's. But Georgiana said, in a letter to Admiral George Preble, that the flag was in her possession during the rebellion.

June 24, 1873

The flag was displayed in the Charleston Naval Yards. Canvas backing was sewn on the flag and one of the first photographs was taken of it.

1876

The flag was loaned to the Navy Department for the Centenial Celebration.

1879

Georgiana Armistead Appleton died in 1879 and left the flag to her son Eben Appleton.

1907

Eben Appleton loaned the flag to the Smithsonian.

1912

Eben Appleton converts the loan of the flag to a gift to the Smithsonian.

1914

Amelia Fowler was commissioned to remove the canvas backing sewn on the flag when it was photographed in 1873 and replace it with the present linen backing.

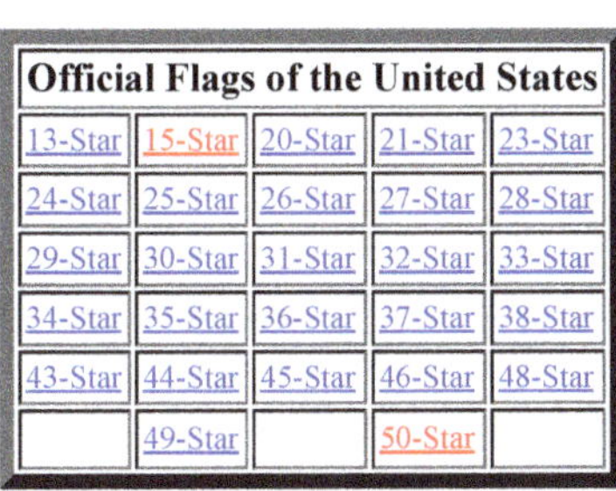

Official Flags of the United States				
13-Star	15-Star	20-Star	21-Star	23-Star
24-Star	25-Star	26-Star	27-Star	28-Star
29-Star	30-Star	31-Star	32-Star	33-Star
34-Star	35-Star	36-Star	37-Star	38-Star
43-Star	44-Star	45-Star	46-Star	48-Star
	49-Star		50-Star	

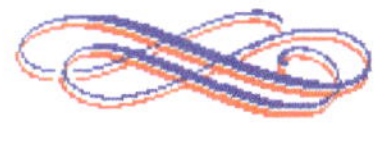

The 1818 Flag, the 20 Star Flag

The 20 Star Flag is available for purchase from my friends at U.S. Flag Depot, Inc.

The 1818 Flag:Realizing that the addition of a new star and new stripe for each new State was impractical, Congress passed the Flag Act of 1818 which returned the flag design to 13 stripes and specified 20 stars for the 20 states.

This Flag became the Official United States Flag on April 13th, 1818. Five stars were added for the admission of Tennessee (the 16th State on June 1st, 1796), Ohio (the 17th State on March 1st, 1803), Louisiana (the 18th State on April 30th, 1812), Indiana (the 19th State on December 11th, 1816), and Mississippi (the 20th State on December 10, 1817), and was to last for just one year. The only President to serve under this flag was James Monroe (1817-1825).

Official Flags of the United States				
13-Star	15-Star	20-Star	21-Star	23-Star
24-Star	25-Star	26-Star	27-Star	28-Star
29-Star	30-Star	31-Star	32-Star	33-Star
34-Star	35-Star	36-Star	37-Star	38-Star
43-Star	44-Star	45-Star	46-Star	48-Star
	49-Star		50-Star	

Search for ⊙ This Site / ◯ The Web   **Search**

Site Search

 **Home Page**] [Table of Contents]

[Historic Flags] [History] [Patriotic Writings]

[Miscellaneous] [& Etcetera]

[Links to Web Sites of Special Interest]

[Comments Welcomed]

The 21-Star Flag

The 21 Star Flag is available for purchase from my friends at U.S. Flag Depot, Inc.

The 21-Star Flag: This Flag became the Official United States Flag on July 4th,1819. A star was added for the admission of Illinois (December 3rd, 1818) and was to last for just one year. The only President to serve under this flag was James Monroe (1817-1825).

Official Flags of the United States				
13-Star	15-Star	20-Star	21-Star	23-Star
24-Star	25-Star	26-Star	27-Star	28-Star
29-Star	30-Star	31-Star	32-Star	33-Star
34-Star	35-Star	36-Star	37-Star	38-Star
43-Star	44-Star	45-Star	46-Star	48-Star
	49-Star		50-Star	

Search for ⦿ This Site ◯ The Web [Search]

Site Search

[Home Page] [Table of Contents]

[Historic Flags] [History] [Patriotic Writings]

The 23-Star Flag

The 23 Star Flag is [available for purchase](#) from my friends at [U.S. Flag Depot, Inc.](#)

The 23-Star Flag: This Flag became the Official United States Flag on July 4th, 1820. Two stars were added for the admission of [Alabama](#) (the 22nd state on December 14th,1819) and [Maine](#) (the 23rd state on March 15, 1820) and was to last for 2 years. The only President to serve under this flag was [James Monroe (1817-1825)](#).

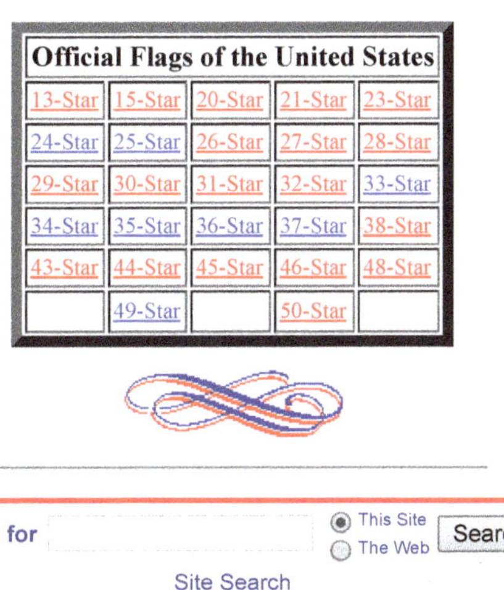

Official Flags of the United States				
[13-Star](#)	[15-Star](#)	[20-Star](#)	[21-Star](#)	[23-Star](#)
[24-Star](#)	[25-Star](#)	[26-Star](#)	[27-Star](#)	[28-Star](#)
[29-Star](#)	[30-Star](#)	[31-Star](#)	[32-Star](#)	[33-Star](#)
[34-Star](#)	[35-Star](#)	[36-Star](#)	[37-Star](#)	[38-Star](#)
[43-Star](#)	[44-Star](#)	[45-Star](#)	[46-Star](#)	[48-Star](#)
	[49-Star](#)		[50-Star](#)	

Search for _______________ ⦿ This Site   ◯ The Web   [Search]

[Site Search](#)

[**Home Page**] [Table of Contents]

[Historic Flags] [History] [Patriotic Writings]

The 24-Star Flag

The 24 Star Flag is available for purchase from my friends at U.S. Flag Depot, Inc.

The 24-Star Flag: This Flag became the Official United States Flag on July 4th,1822. A star was added for the admission of Missouri (August 10th, 1821) and was to last for fourteen years. The Presidents who served under this flag included James Monroe (1817-1825), John Quincy Adams (1825-1829), and Andrew Jackson (1829-1837).

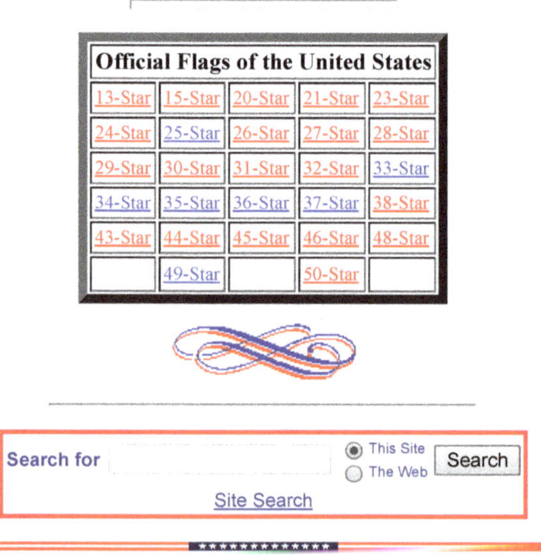

Official Flags of the United States				
13-Star	15-Star	20-Star	21-Star	23-Star
24-Star	25-Star	26-Star	27-Star	28-Star
29-Star	30-Star	31-Star	32-Star	33-Star
34-Star	35-Star	36-Star	37-Star	38-Star
43-Star	44-Star	45-Star	46-Star	48-Star
	49-Star		50-Star	

Search for   ◉ This Site   ◯ The Web   **Search**

Site Search

[Home Page] [Table of Contents]

[Historic Flags] [History] [Patriotic Writings]

The 26-Star Flag

The 26 Star Flag is available for purchase from my friends at U.S. Flag Depot, Inc.

The 26-Star Flag: This Flag became the Official United States Flag on July 4th, 1837. A star was added for the admission of Michigan (January 26th,1837) and was to last for 8 years. The four Presidents to serve under this flag were; Martin Van Buren (1837-1841), William Henry Harrison (1841), John Tyler (1841-1845), and James Polk (1845-1849).

Official Flags of the United States				
13-Star	15-Star	20-Star	21-Star	23-Star
24-Star	25-Star	26-Star	27-Star	28-Star
29-Star	30-Star	31-Star	32-Star	33-Star
34-Star	35-Star	36-Star	37-Star	38-Star
43-Star	44-Star	45-Star	46-Star	48-Star
	49-Star		50-Star	

Search for ⦿ This Site ◯ The Web [Search]

Site Search

[Home Page] [Table of Contents]

[Historic Flags] [History] [Patriotic Writings]

[Miscellaneous] [& Etcetera]

[Links to Web Sites of Special Interest]

[Comments Welcomed]

The 27-Star Flag

The 27 Star Flag is available for purchase from my friends at U.S. Flag Depot, Inc.

The 27-Star Flag: This Flag became the Official United States Flag on July 4th, 1845. A star was added for the admission of Florida and was to last for only 1 year. The only President to serve under this flag was James Polk (1845-1849).

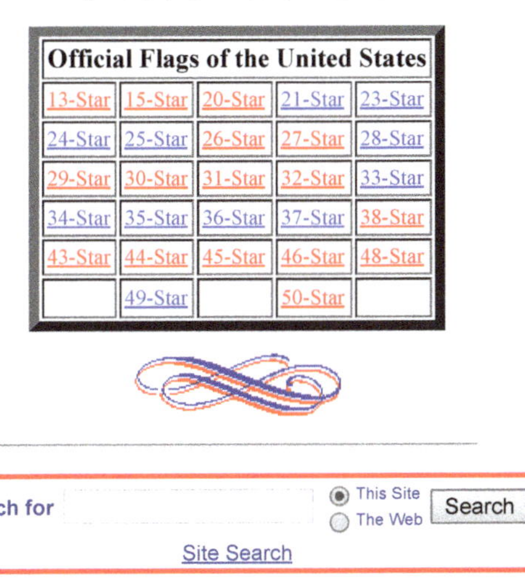

Official Flags of the United States				
13-Star	15-Star	20-Star	21-Star	23-Star
24-Star	25-Star	26-Star	27-Star	28-Star
29-Star	30-Star	31-Star	32-Star	33-Star
34-Star	35-Star	36-Star	37-Star	38-Star
43-Star	44-Star	45-Star	46-Star	48-Star
	49-Star		50-Star	

Search for [______________]   ⦿ This Site   ◯ The Web   [Search]

Site Search

[Home Page] [Table of Contents]

[Historic Flags] [History] [Patriotic Writings]

The 28-Star Flag

The 28 Star Flag is available for purchase from my friends at U.S. Flag Depot, Inc.

The 28-Star Flag: This Flag became the Official United States Flag on July 4th, 1846. A star was added for the admission of Texas (December 29th, 1845) and was to last for only 1 year. The only President to serve under this flag was James Polk (1845-1849).

Official Flags of the United States				
13-Star	15-Star	20-Star	21-Star	23-Star
24-Star	25-Star	26-Star	27-Star	28-Star
29-Star	30-Star	31-Star	32-Star	33-Star
34-Star	35-Star	36-Star	37-Star	38-Star
43-Star	44-Star	45-Star	46-Star	48-Star
	49-Star		50-Star	

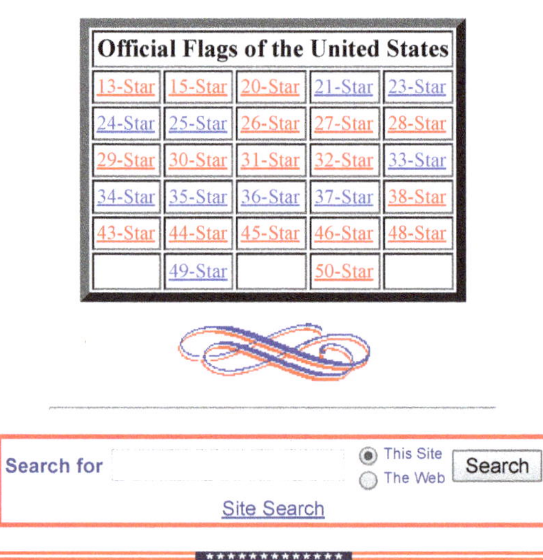

Search for [   ] ◉ This Site ○ The Web [Search]

Site Search

Home Page | [Table of Contents]

[Historic Flags] [History] [Patriotic Writings]

The 29-Star Flag

The 29 Star Flag is available for purchase from my friends at U.S. Flag Depot, Inc.

The 29-Star Flag: This Flag became the Official United States Flag on July 4th, 1847. A star was added for the admission of Iowa (December 28th, 1846) and was to last for only 1 year. The only President to serve under this flag was James Polk (1845-1849).

Official Flags of the United States				
13-Star	15-Star	20-Star	21-Star	23-Star
24-Star	25-Star	26-Star	27-Star	28-Star
29-Star	30-Star	31-Star	32-Star	33-Star
34-Star	35-Star	36-Star	37-Star	38-Star
43-Star	44-Star	45-Star	46-Star	48-Star
	49-Star		50-Star	

Search for   ( ) This Site ( ) The Web [Search]

Site Search

[Home Page] [Table of Contents]

[Historic Flags] [History] [Patriotic Writings]

The 30-Star Flag

The 30 Star Flag is available for purchase from my friends at U.S. Flag Depot, Inc.

The 30-Star Flag: This Flag became the Official United States Flag on July 4th, 1848. A star was added for the admission of Wisconsin (May 29th, 1848) and was to last for 3 years. The three Presidents to serve under this flag were; James Polk (1845-1849), Zachary Taylor (1849-1850),and Millard Fillmore (1850-1853).

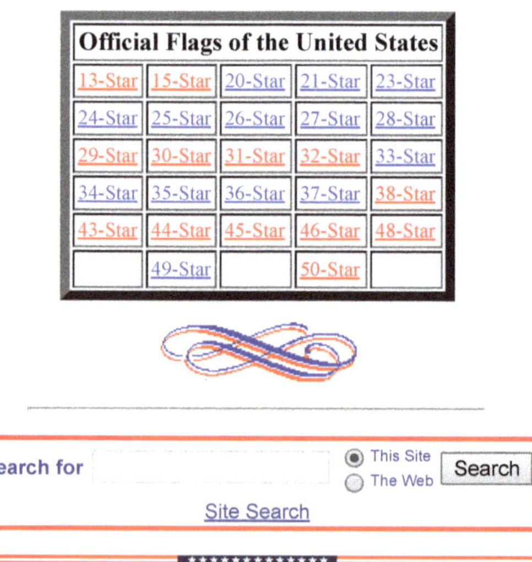

Official Flags of the United States				
13-Star	15-Star	20-Star	21-Star	23-Star
24-Star	25-Star	26-Star	27-Star	28-Star
29-Star	30-Star	31-Star	32-Star	33-Star
34-Star	35-Star	36-Star	37-Star	38-Star
43-Star	44-Star	45-Star	46-Star	48-Star
	49-Star		50-Star	

Search for [______________] ⦿ This Site ◯ The Web [Search]

Site Search

Home Page] [Table of Contents]

[Historic Flags] [History] [Patriotic Writings]

The 31-Star Flag

The 31 Star Flag is available for purchase from my friends at U.S. Flag Depot, Inc.

The 31-Star Flag: This Flag became the Official United States Flag on July 4th 1851. A star was added for the admission of California (September 9th, 1850) and was to last for seven years. The three Presidents who served under this flag were; Millard Fillmore (1850-1853), Franklin Pierce (1853-1857), and James Buchanan (1857-1861).

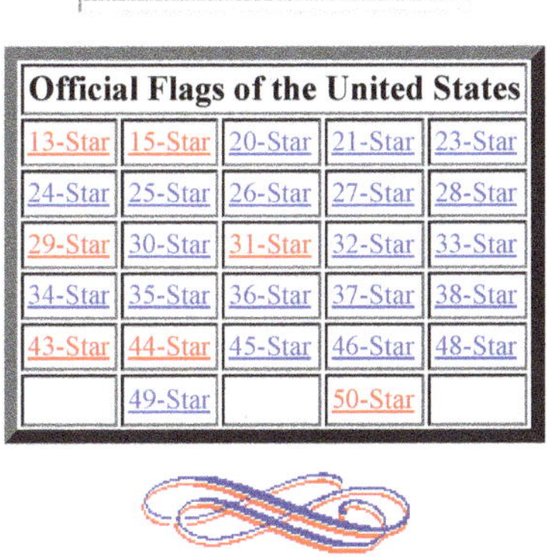

Official Flags of the United States				
13-Star	15-Star	20-Star	21-Star	23-Star
24-Star	25-Star	26-Star	27-Star	28-Star
29-Star	30-Star	31-Star	32-Star	33-Star
34-Star	35-Star	36-Star	37-Star	38-Star
43-Star	44-Star	45-Star	46-Star	48-Star
	49-Star		50-Star	

Search for   ⦿ This Site   ◯ The Web   **Search**

Site Search

[Home Page] [Table of Contents]

[Historic Flags] [History] [Patriotic Writings]

The 32-Star Flag

The 32 Star Flag is available for purchase from my friends at U.S. Flag Depot, Inc.

The 32-Star Flag: This Flag became the Official United States Flag on July 4th, 1858. A star was added for the admission of Minnesota (May 11, 1858) and was to last for just one year. The only President to serve under this flag was James Buchanan (1857-1861).

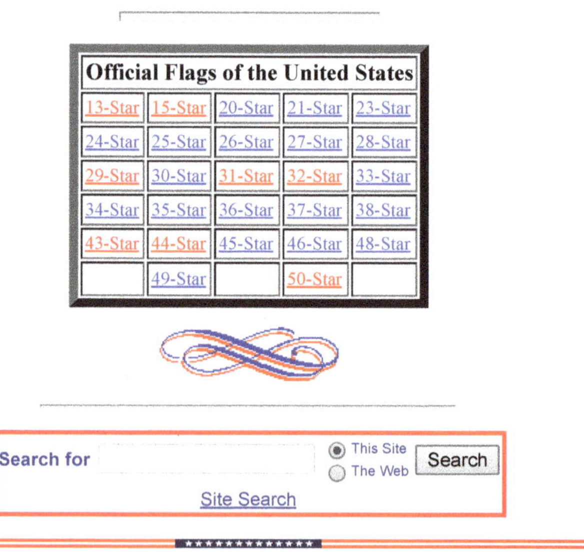

Official Flags of the United States				
13-Star	15-Star	20-Star	21-Star	23-Star
24-Star	25-Star	26-Star	27-Star	28-Star
29-Star	30-Star	31-Star	32-Star	33-Star
34-Star	35-Star	36-Star	37-Star	38-Star
43-Star	44-Star	45-Star	46-Star	48-Star
	49-Star		50-Star	

Search for ⦿ This Site ◯ The Web **Search**

Site Search

Home Page | [Table of Contents]

[Historic Flags] [History] [Patriotic Writings]

The 33-Star Flag

The 33 Star Flag is available for purchase from my friends at U.S. Flag Depot, Inc.

The 33-Star Flag: This Flag became the Official United States Flag on July 4th, 1859. A star was added for the admission of Oregon (February 14, 1859) and was to last for 2 years. The two Presidents to serve under this flag were James Buchanan (1857-1861) and Abraham Lincoln (1861-1865).

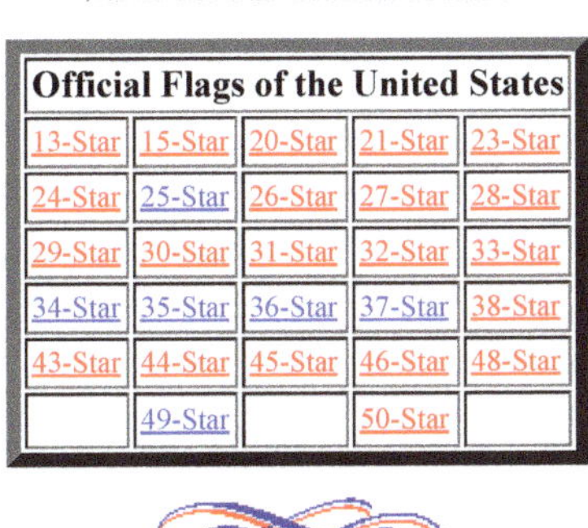

Official Flags of the United States				
13-Star	15-Star	20-Star	21-Star	23-Star
24-Star	25-Star	26-Star	27-Star	28-Star
29-Star	30-Star	31-Star	32-Star	33-Star
34-Star	35-Star	36-Star	37-Star	38-Star
43-Star	44-Star	45-Star	46-Star	48-Star
	49-Star		50-Star	

Search for [________]   ⦿ This Site   ◯ The Web   [Search]

Site Search

[Home Page] [Table of Contents]

[Historic Flags] [History] [Patriotic Writings]

The 34-Star Flag

The 34 Star Flag is available for purchase from my friends at U.S. Flag Depot, Inc.

The 34-Star Flag: This Flag became the Official United States Flag on July 4th, 1861. A star was added for the admission of Kansas (January 29th, 1861) and was to last for 2 years. The only President to serve under this flag was Abraham Lincoln (1861-1865).

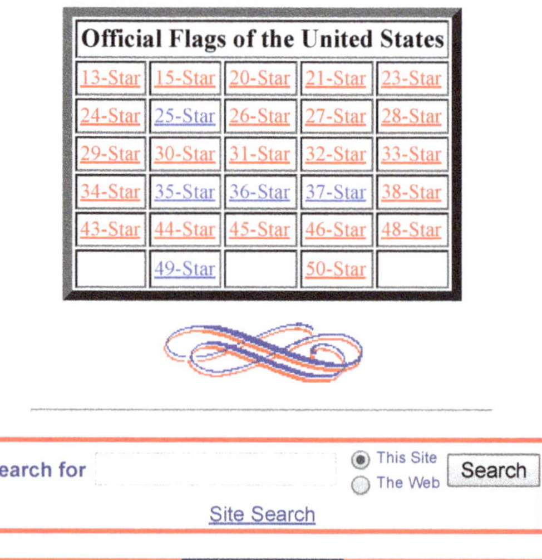

Official Flags of the United States				
13-Star	15-Star	20-Star	21-Star	23-Star
24-Star	25-Star	26-Star	27-Star	28-Star
29-Star	30-Star	31-Star	32-Star	33-Star
34-Star	35-Star	36-Star	37-Star	38-Star
43-Star	44-Star	45-Star	46-Star	48-Star
	49-Star		50-Star	

Search for [____________] ⊙ This Site ○ The Web [Search]

Site Search

[Home Page] [Table of Contents]

[Historic Flags] [History] [Patriotic Writings]

The 35-Star Flag

The 35 Star Flag is available for purchase from my friends at U.S. Flag Depot, Inc.

The 35-Star Flag: This Flag became the Official United States Flag on July 4th, 1863. A star was added for the admission of West Virginia (June 20th, 1863) and was to last for 2 years. The two Presidents to serve under this flag were Abraham Lincoln (1861-1865) and Andrew Johnson (1865-1869).

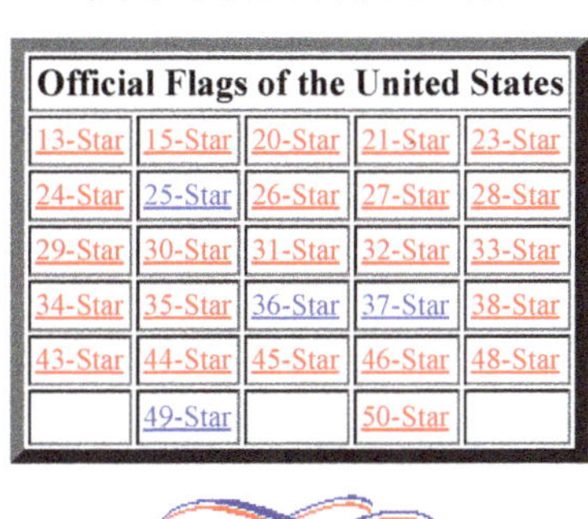

Official Flags of the United States				
13-Star	15-Star	20-Star	21-Star	23-Star
24-Star	25-Star	26-Star	27-Star	28-Star
29-Star	30-Star	31-Star	32-Star	33-Star
34-Star	35-Star	36-Star	37-Star	38-Star
43-Star	44-Star	45-Star	46-Star	48-Star
	49-Star		50-Star	

Search for [   ] ◉ This Site ◯ The Web [Search]

Site Search

[Home Page] [Table of Contents]

[Historic Flags] [History] [Patriotic Writings]

The 36-Star Flag

The 36 Star Flag is available for purchase from my friends at U.S. Flag Depot, Inc.

The 36-Star Flag: This Flag became the Official United States Flag on July 4th, 1865. A star was added for the admission of Nevada (October 31st, 1864) and was to last for 2 years. The only President to serve under this flag was Andrew Johnson (1865-1869).

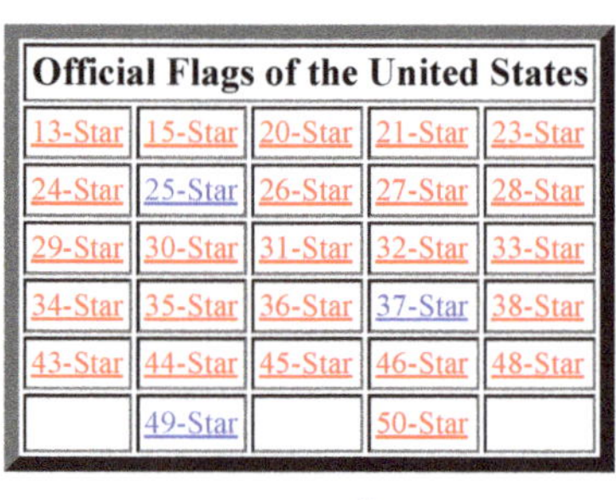

Official Flags of the United States				
13-Star	15-Star	20-Star	21-Star	23-Star
24-Star	25-Star	26-Star	27-Star	28-Star
29-Star	30-Star	31-Star	32-Star	33-Star
34-Star	35-Star	36-Star	37-Star	38-Star
43-Star	44-Star	45-Star	46-Star	48-Star
	49-Star		50-Star	

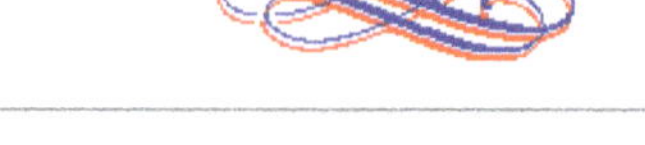

Site Search

[Home Page] [Table of Contents]

[Historic Flags] [History] [Patriotic Writings]

The 37-Star Flag

The 37 Star Flag is available for purchase from my friends at U.S. Flag Depot, Inc.

The 37-Star Flag: This Flag became the Official United States Flag on July 4th 1867. A star was added for the admission of Nebraska (March 1st,1867) and was to last for ten years. The three Presidents who served under this flag were; Andrew Johnson (1865-1869), Ulysses S. Grant (1869-1877), and Rutherford B. Hayes (1877-1881).

Official Flags of the United States				
13-Star	15-Star	20-Star	21-Star	23-Star
24-Star	25-Star	26-Star	27-Star	28-Star
29-Star	30-Star	31-Star	32-Star	33-Star
34-Star	35-Star	36-Star	37-Star	38-Star
43-Star	44-Star	45-Star	46-Star	48-Star
	49-Star		50-Star	

Search for [____________] ⦿ This Site ◯ The Web   [Search]

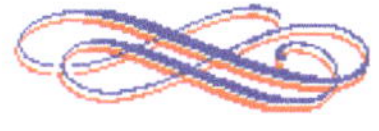

Site Search

[Home Page] [Table of Contents]

[Historic Flags] [History] [Patriotic Writings]

The 38-Star Flag

The 38 Star Flag is available for purchase from my friends at U.S. Flag Depot, Inc.

The 38-Star Flag: This Flag became the Official United States Flag on July 4th, 1877. A star was added for the admission of Colorado (August 1st 1876) and was to last for 13 years. The five Presidents to serve under this flag were; Rutherford B. Hayes (1877-1881), James A. Garfield (1881), Chester A. Arthur (1881-1885), Grover Cleveland (1885-1889), and Benjamin Harrison (1889-1893).

Official Flags of the United States				
13-Star	15-Star	20-Star	21-Star	23-Star
24-Star	25-Star	26-Star	27-Star	28-Star
29-Star	30-Star	31-Star	32-Star	33-Star
34-Star	35-Star	36-Star	37-Star	38-Star
43-Star	44-Star	45-Star	46-Star	48-Star
	49-Star		50-Star	

Search for   ◉ This Site   ○ The Web   [Search]

Site Search

[Home Page] [Table of Contents]

[Historic Flags] [History] [Patriotic Writings]

The 43-Star Flag

The 43 Star Flag is available for purchase from my friends at U.S. Flag Depot, Inc.

The 43-Star Flag: This Flag became the Official United States Flag on July 4th, 1890. Five stars were added for the admission of North Dakota (the 39th State on November 2nd,1889), South Dakota (the 40th State on November 2nd,1889), Montana (the 41st State on November 8th,1889), Washington (the 42nd State on November 11th,1889), and Idaho (the 43rd State on July 3rd, 1890) and was to last for just 1 year. The only President to serve under this flag was Benjamin Harrison (1889-1893).

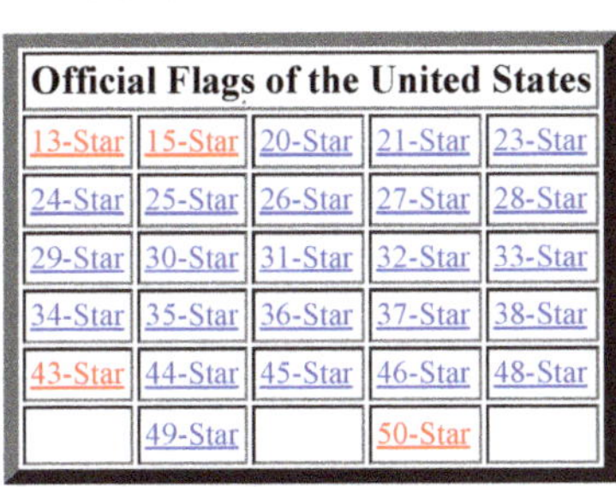

Official Flags of the United States				
13-Star	15-Star	20-Star	21-Star	23-Star
24-Star	25-Star	26-Star	27-Star	28-Star
29-Star	30-Star	31-Star	32-Star	33-Star
34-Star	35-Star	36-Star	37-Star	38-Star
43-Star	44-Star	45-Star	46-Star	48-Star
	49-Star		50-Star	

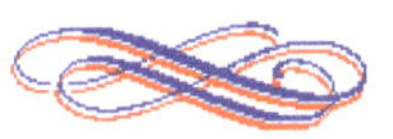

Search for [   ]   ◉ This Site   ○ The Web   [Search]

Site Search

[Home Page] [Table of Contents]

The 44-Star Flag

The 44 Star Flag is available for purchase from my friends at U.S. Flag Depot, Inc.

The 44-Star Flag: This Flag became the Official United States Flag on July 4th, 1891. A star was added for the admission of Wyoming (July 10, 1890) and was to last for 5 years. The Presidents to serve under this flag were Benjamin Harrison (1889-1893) and Grover Cleveland (1893-1897).

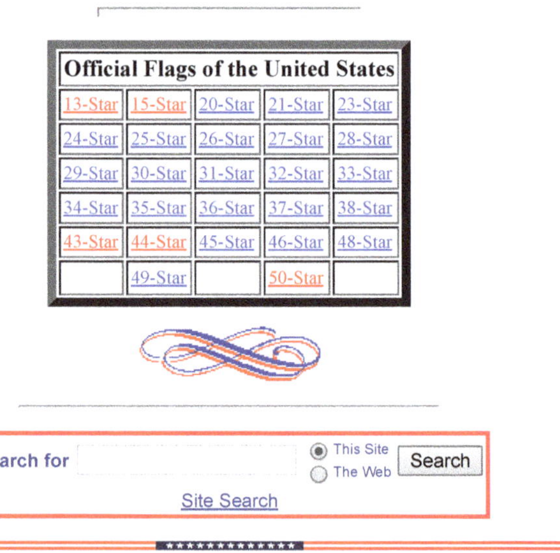

Official Flags of the United States				
13-Star	15-Star	20-Star	21-Star	23-Star
24-Star	25-Star	26-Star	27-Star	28-Star
29-Star	30-Star	31-Star	32-Star	33-Star
34-Star	35-Star	36-Star	37-Star	38-Star
43-Star	44-Star	45-Star	46-Star	48-Star
	49-Star		50-Star	

Search for [   ]   ⦿ This Site ◯ The Web   [Search]

Site Search

[**Home Page**] [Table of Contents]

[Historic Flags] [History] [Patriotic Writings]

The 45-Star Flag

The 45 Star Flag is available for purchase from my friends at U.S. Flag Depot, Inc.

The 45-Star Flag: This Flag became the Official United States Flag on July 4th, 1896. A star was added for the admission of Utah on January 4th, 1896, and was to last for 12 years. The Presidents to serve under this flag were Grover Cleveland (1893-1897), William McKinley (1897-1901),and Theodore Roosevelt (1901-1909).

Official Flags of the United States				
13-Star	15-Star	20-Star	21-Star	23-Star
24-Star	25-Star	26-Star	27-Star	28-Star
29-Star	30-Star	31-Star	32-Star	33-Star
34-Star	35-Star	36-Star	37-Star	38-Star
43-Star	44-Star	45-Star	46-Star	48-Star
	49-Star		50-Star	

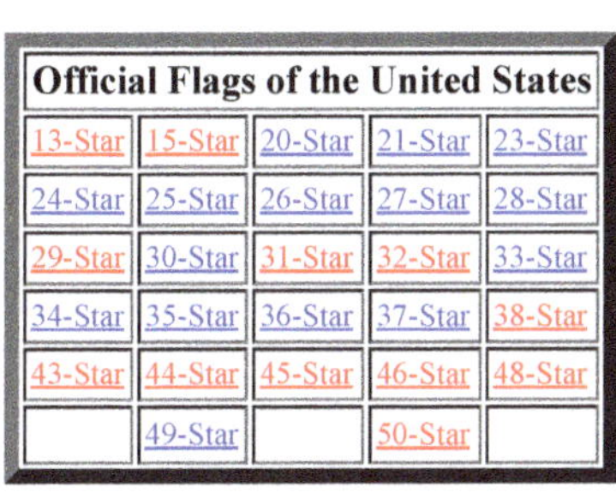

Search for   ⦿ This Site   ◯ The Web   [Search]

Site Search

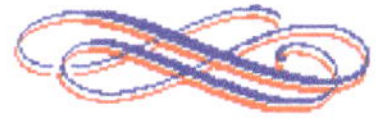

[Home Page] [Table of Contents]

[Historic Flags] [History] [Patriotic Writings]

The 46 Star Flag

The 46 Star Flag is available for purchase from my friends at U.S. Flag Depot, Inc.

The 46 Star Flag: On July 4,1908, the U.S. flag grew to 46 stars with the addition to the Union of Oklahoma (November 16, 1907). Theodore Roosevelt (1901-1909) and William H. Taft (1909-1913) served as President under the 46 star flag. This was the official flag for 4 years.

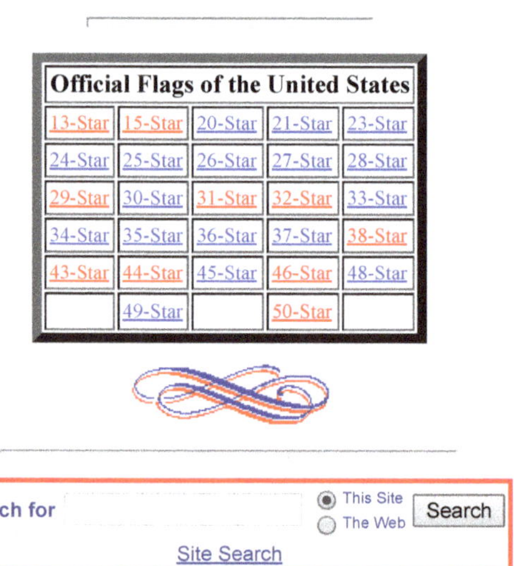

Official Flags of the United States				
13-Star	15-Star	20-Star	21-Star	23-Star
24-Star	25-Star	26-Star	27-Star	28-Star
29-Star	30-Star	31-Star	32-Star	33-Star
34-Star	35-Star	36-Star	37-Star	38-Star
43-Star	44-Star	45-Star	46-Star	48-Star
	49-Star		50-Star	

Search for ⦿ This Site ◯ The Web [Search]

Site Search

[Home Page] [Table of Contents]

[Historic Flags] [History] [Patriotic Writings]

The 50 Star Flag

Top quality 50 Star Flags are available for purchase from my friends at U.S. Flag Depot, Inc.

50-Star Flag: Executive Order of President Eisenhower dated August 21, 1959 - provided for the arrangement of the stars in nine rows of stars staggered horizon tally and eleven rows of stars staggered vertically. This is the current flag of the United States. Hawaii was admitted as the 50th state on August 21st, 1959. The 27th flag of the United States became the official flag on July 4th, 1960. Nine presidents have served under this flag; Dwight D. Eisenhower (1953-1961), John F. Kennedy (1961-1963), Lyndon B. Johnson (1963-1969), Richard M. Nixon (1969-1974), Gerald R. Ford (1974-1977), Jimmy Carter (1977-1981), Ronald W. Reagan (1981-1989), George Bush (1989-1993), William J. Clinton (1993-2001) and George W. Bush (2001-present)*.

* Bush is only the fourth President to lose the popular vote but win the Presidency by means of the Electoral College. Andrew Jackson and Grover Cleveland suffered the same setback as Al Gore, but went on to win in a later election. Samuel Tilden, the people's choice in 1876, is the only member of this elite group who shunned a comeback. History will show to which group Al Gore will belong, having won the election by some half million votes but losing in the Electoral College.

Official Flags of the United States				
13-Star	15-Star	20-Star	21-Star	23-Star
24-Star	25-Star	26-Star	27-Star	28-Star
29-Star	30-Star	31-Star	32-Star	33-Star
34-Star	35-Star	36-Star	37-Star	38-Star
43-Star	44-Star	45-Star	46-Star	48-Star
	49-Star		50-Star	

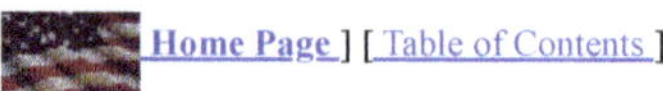

Site Search

[Home Page] [Table of Contents]

[Historic Flags] [History] [Patriotic Writings]

[Miscellaneous] [& Etcetera]

[Links to Web Sites of Special Interest]

[Comments Welcomed]

Veteran's Traveling Flag Display and Museum Presentation

By Mickey L, Dennis

This flag display is in honor of all military members, past and present, who have served and are now serving our nation in times of war and peace. This display is primarily for the education and information of teachers, students, and the general public, to better understand the history of our military and their service to our nation. This display is not intended to be an endorsement of any military service or a recruiting tool for any service.

The American flag always leads any group or line of flags, The stars of the American flag always lead the line regardless of the direction of the line. The MIA/POW flag always follows the American flag in a line or group as an honor to those still missing in action and/or still POW. It is believed that there is no more living MIA/POW in captivity. The next set of flags represents the major conflicts that our nation has been involved in from WWII to present. The first flag is an Iraq freedom flag, handmade in Baghdad, in January 2003. The Afghanistan flag, is next and followed by the flag of Bosnia. These are the three countries where our military is presently serving under combat condition. The next flag is the desert storm flag, which still covers the present conflict in Iraq and Afghanistan. Congress has not terminated the Desert Storm Action period. The next flag is the flag of South Vietnam for the country of South Vietnam at that time. It is the flag under which most of the people of our Asian community lived under at that time. It is authorized by proclamation to be used here to represent the country of South Vietnam at that time in History. The next is the Vietnam Veterans War Commemorative flag, which shows the map of South Vietnam and the major units involved in the War action. This period from 1955 through 1976,covered all areas of South East Asia. The next flag is the Korean War commemorative flag, The Korean War was a police Action, from 1950 through 1953, which has not yet ended, with our military still serving in Korea today. The last flag of this group is the WWII Commemorative flag. Our Military are still serving under NATO in Europe, and in other areas of the World from the actions of WWII. The WWI commemorative flag is not included because there is a problem obtaining that flag. We do have some WWI Vets still alive in South Dakota. The next group, are the flags of our Armed Services in the order of their conception by congress. The United States Army, United States Marines, and United States Merchants Marines, were all authorized in 1776. The United States Navy was authorized much

Sketch in the diary of Ezra Stiles (detail)

American; 1783 Apr. 24; Original at Yale University.

Original is an ink line drawing over some faint pencil sketching. The available illustration is only a detail so the exact number of stripes is not shown. His diary describes it as having "The stripes red and white, with azure field in the upper part charged with 13 stars." He also describes the arms as those of the US but in this he erred.

Stars: 13 six-pointed stars disposed around the arms of Pennsylvania, 3 and 3 on either side at the top, 2 and 2 in the center and 2 and 1 at the bottom, above the motto.

Canton: extends to the 6th stripe.

Stripes: presumably there are 13.

Image source: Furlong, pg. 144

Diploma Sketch for Society of Cincinnati by Pierre L'Enfant (detail)

American; 1783 June 10; Original is in the Library of Congress, owned by the Society of the Cincinnati.

The original is a monochrome watercolor.

Stars: 13 five-pointed dark stars on a light canton arranged in an oval.

Canton: extends to the 7th stripe. "Rests" on a W stripe.

Stripes: 13 alternate dark and light, 7 dark and 6 light.

Image source: Cooper, pg. 5

Guilford Court House Flag
American; 1791-1792? Original at the North Carolina Hall of History.
Grace Rogers Cooper assessed this flag as being 18th century but probably after 1795 due to the evidence of at least 14 stripes and the conjecture that there were probably more stars. Experts have agreed with her assessment. However, ignoring any conjecture and considering only the physical evidence of 14 stripes and 13 stars, one cannot escape the equally likely possibility that the flag was only what it appears today, with a 14th stripe added for Vermont which was admitted in 1791 but before Kentucky was admitted in 1792. This flag is very unusually long and narrow with a very long canton. Even if it was a 15 star 15 stripe flag, it could date as early as 1792 when the 15th state was admitted. Coloring is suggestive of another Carolina flag, that of the Warship South Carolina (see #34, below).
Stars: 13 eight-pointed B stars on a W canton arranged 4-3-4 (staggered) with 2 placed at the fly end of the canton (staggered vertically).
Canton: extends to the 8th stripe. "Rests" on a B stripe.
Stripes: 12 B-R complete and small pieces of two additional at the bottom, making 7 of each.
Image source: Richardson, pg. 211

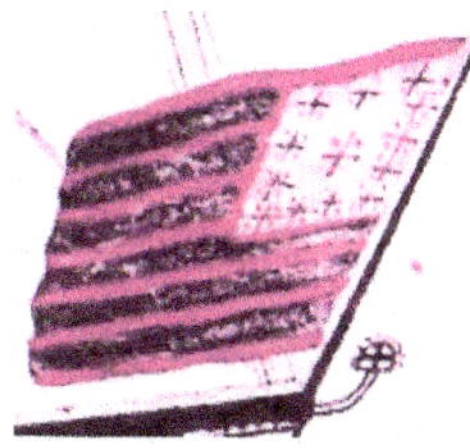

South Carolina by Jon. Phippen (warship painting detail)
American; 1793; Original at the Peabody Museum.
Coloring is suggestive of another Carolina flag, that associated with Guilford Court House, North Carolina (see #33, above).
Stars: 13 unusual B four-pointed stars with R dots between the points on a W canton arranged with 12 in a square and one in the center.
Canton: extends half way into the 8th stripe and is W bordered on all but the hoist side in R. "Rests" half way into a B stripe.
Stripes: 13 R-B, 7 R and 6 B.
Image source: Mastai, pg. 65

Tableau de Tous les Pavillons que l'on Arbore sur les Vaisseaux dans les Quatre Parties du Monde (detail)
German; 1793; Original at the Mariner's Museum.
Also known as the Lotter Flag Sheet. The flag illustration is hand colored.
Stars: 13 six-pointed W stars on a B canton arranged 3-2-3-2-3 (staggered).

Beauvais Tapestry (detail)
French; 1783; Original owned by the National Trust of Great Britain.
The original was commissioned in 1783 by the King of France and was intended to be a gift to George Washington. The French Revolution intervened such that it was never delivered.
Stars: 13 five-pointed W stars on a B canton arranged 3-3-3-3-1 (even with last star centered) plus one gold Fleur-di-lis at the center top of the canton. Stars are set somewhat high on the long canton.
Canton: extends to the 10th stripe. "Rests" on a W stripe.
Stripes: 12 alternate W-R, 6 W and 6 R. Flag is folded at top in image and presumably there is a 13th W stripe at the top.
Image source: Mastai, pg. 36

Carrington Bowles' Book of Flags (detail)
British; 1783; Original at Brown University. The flag illustration is hand colored.
Stars: 13 six-pointed W stars on a B canton arranged 3-2-3-2-3 (staggered).
Canton: extends to the 5th stripe. "Rests" on a W stripe.
Stripes: 13 R-W, 7 R and 6 W.
Image source: Furlong, pg. 150

Francis Bailey's Pocket Almanac of 1784 (detail)
American; 1783; Original in the Library of Congress.
Original is an engraved line drawing but is "heraldically hatched" to indicate color.
Stars: 13 probably five-pointed W stars on a B canton arranged 4-5-4 (staggered).
Canton: extends down to the 7th stripe. "Rests" on a W stripe.
Stripes: 13 R-W, 7 R and 6 W.
Image source: Furlong, pg. 152

. 1. U.S. Flag in engraving made at Philadelphia for the *Columbian Magazine* entitled "A View of the Town of Boston, the Capital of New England".
American; dated December, 1787.
The flag in this scene is possibly an artist's impression of the Fort Independence Flag (See flag number 8, above).
Stars: 13 5-pointed dark on light, arranged in three rows of 5-4-4 (staggered).
Canton: Light, extends to the 6th stripe. "Rests" on a W stripe.
Stripes: 11 dark and white, 5 dark and 6 white.
Image Source: Matthew Larsen.
Note: This image was added subsequent to the original article, hence the numerical designation 26.1.

Battle of Princeton by John Trumbull (painting detail)
American; 1787-1797; Original at Yale University.
Stars: The stars are somewhat indistinct but appear to be 13 four-pointed W stars on a B canton arranged in a square of 12 with one in the center.
Canton: extends to the 6th stripe. "Rests" on a R stripe.
Stripes: 13 R-W, 7 R and 6 W.
Image source: McDowell, pg. 2-3

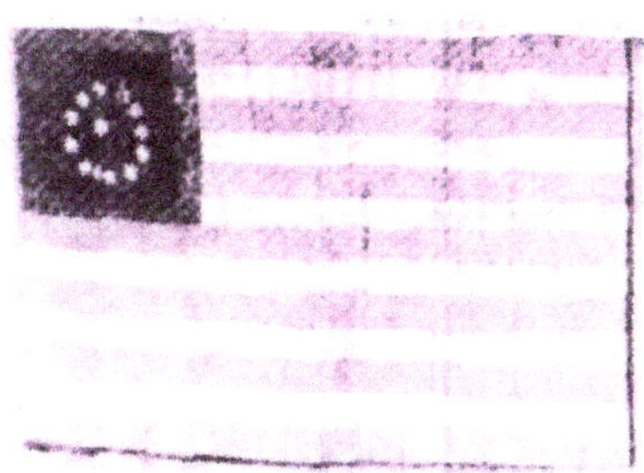

Society of Pewterers Flag, New York (canton detail)
American; 1788 July 23; Original at the New York Historical Society.
Flag shows the arms of the Pewterers as well as a view of a Pewterer's shop in production and a poem. It was used in the Grand Federal Procession held in New York City to celebrate the adoption of the US Constitution. It is fringed.
Stars: 13 W stars on a B canton arranged in a circle of 12 with one in the center. The stars have various numbers of points ranging from 5 to 8, apparently 3 five-pointed, 3 six-pointed, 5 seven-pointed and 2 eight-pointed.
Canton: extends to the 6th stripe. "Rests" on a R stripe.
Stripes: 13 R-W, 7 R and 6 W.
Image source: Richardson, pg. 32

3. U.S. Ensign on flag chart entitled *A View of the Flaggs that are to be found at Sea in all Parts of the World* published in London by Laurie & Whittle.

British; dated May 12, 1794.

Stars: 13 5-pointed W, arranged in rows of 3-2-3-2-3 (staggered).

Canton: Blue, extends to the 7th stripe. "Rests" on a W stripe.

Stripes: 13 red and white, 7 R and 6 W.

Image Source: Matthew Larsen.

Note: This image was added subsequent to the original article, hence the numerical designation 35.3.

Washington Reviewing the Western Army by Frederick Kemmelmeyer (painting detail)

American; 1795; Original at the Henry Francis DuPont Winterthur Museum.

Stars: 10 W stars on a B canton, arranged 4-3-3 (even). Due to small scale, stars are multi-pointed (probably greater than 5) but indistinct.

Canton: extends to the 9th stripe. "Rests" on a R stripe.

Stripes: 19 W-R, 10 W and 9 R.

Image source: Van Every, pg. 56

Canton: extends to the 6th stripe. "Rests" on a R stripe.
Stripes: 13 R-B-W, 5 R, 4 W and 4 B.
Image source: Quaife, pg. 56

1. Flag of the American States on map of "North America", engraved by Samuel John Neele (1758 - 1824), published by G.G. & J. Robinson, London.
British; dated 1793.
The map and flag are hand colored.
Stars: 13 multipointed (probably intended to be 6-pointed) W, arranged in rows of 3-2-3-2-3 (staggered).
Canton: B, extends to the 7th stripe. "Rests" on a W stripe.
Stripes: 13 R and W, 7 R and 6 W.
Image Source: Daniel I. Caplan, MD.
Note: This image was added subsequent to the original article, hence the numerical designation 35.1.

2. U.S. America (Flag) on chart from Rees' Encyclopedia.
British; dated 1794.
This chart was purchased separately from the encyclopedia it purports to come from. Source is assumed.
Stars: 13 6-pointed W, arranged in rows of 3-2-3-2-3 (staggered).
Canton: hatched B, extends to the center of the 8th stripe. Does not "rest" on any stripe; rather it extends to the center of the flag.
Stripes: 13 R and W, 7 R and 6 W.
Image Source: Matthew Larsen.
Note: This image was added subsequent to the original article, hence the numerical designation 35.2.

Continental Congress Gold Medal Awarded to Daniel Morgan for Cowpens (detail)
French; 1789; Original owned by the United States Mint.
Engraved by A. Dupré Paris. This medal shows at least three US Flags, two as described below and one in the background that may have just stars in the canton. The British flag is incorrectly shown as the English arms, three lions.
Stars: indistinct number arranged in arc over US Arms in canton. Number of points indeterminable.
Canton: extends to the 5th stripe. "Rests" on a dark stripe.
Stripes: 13 alternate light and dark, 7 light and 6 dark.
Image source: Richardson, pg. 82

1. U.S. Flag in engraving made at Boston for the *Massachusetts Magazine* entitled "A North View of Castle William in the Harbour of Boston".
American; dated May, 1789.
The flag in this scene is presumably an artist's impression of the Fort Independence Flag (See flag number 8, above).
Stars: 13 multipointed (probably intended to be 5- or 6-pointed) dark on light, arranged in four rows of 5-3-3-3 (staggered).
Canton: Light, extends to the 9th stripe. "Rests" on a W stripe.
Stripes: 13 dark and white, 7 dark and 6 white.
Image Source: Matthew Larsen; original is in the Library of Congress.
Note: This image was added subsequent to the original article, hence the numerical designation 29.1.

"L'Hommage de l'Amerique a la France" Fabric Design Print (detail)
French; 1790; Original in the Smithsonian Institution.
This is a copy of a 1786 design that has a slightly different flag design. The earlier print is described as having 13 dark stars arranged 4-5-4 on a light canton and 13 dark and light stripes.
Stars: 12 five-pointed dark stars on a light canton arranged crudely to approximate a square of eleven with one in the center.
Canton: extends to the 11th stripe. "Rests" on a very dark stripe.
Stripes: 21 alternate light, darker and very dark, 7 light, 7 darker and 7 very dark.
Image source: Cooper, pg. ii

Fort Washington by Jonathan Heart (sketch detail)
American; 1790; Lithograph copy at the Chicago Historical Society.
The lithograph is inscribed "Drawn by Capt. Jona. Heart U.S.A. 1790." and "Oncken's Lithography, Cincinnati, O." Lithography is a nineteenth century technology. Although the original is probably in color, the illustration is only given in monochrome. The text states the top and bottom stripes are red.
Stars: very indistinct, appears to be 12 or 13 light stars on a dark canton arranged in horizontal rows. Points indeterminable.
Canton: extends to the 5th stripe. "Rests" on a W stripe.
Stripes: 11 alternate dark and light, 6 dark and 5 light.
Image source: Furlong, pg. 155

Stars: 13 multipointed (probably intended to be 5- or 6-pointed) dark on light, arranged in three rows of 5-5-3 (staggered) on one and 4-5-4 (staggered) on the other.
Canton: Light, extends to the 9th stripe and one and to the 7th on the other. "Rests" on a W stripe.
Stripes: 13 dark and white, 7 dark and 6 white.
Image Source: Dr. Henry Moeller.
Note: This image was added subsequent to the original article, hence the numerical designation 24.1.

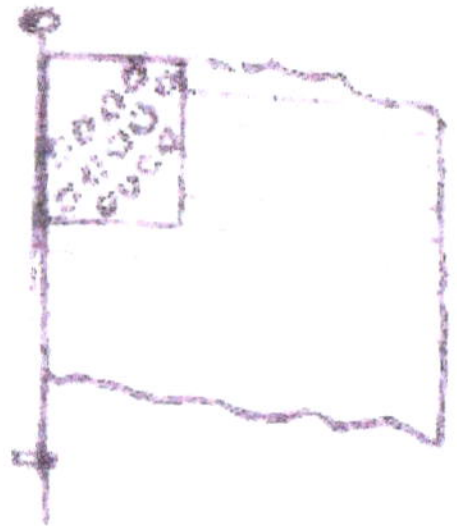

Plan of Fort Harmar (sketch detail)
American; 1786; Original at the William L. Clements Library.
Original is a crude ink line drawing.
Stars: 13 outlined on the canton arranged in diagonal (from lower hoist to upper fly) rows of 4-5-4 (diagonally staggered). The stars are small but it appears some are five-pointed and some may be six-pointed.
Canton: extends to the 5th stripe.
Stripes: 10 stripes.
Image source: Furlong, pg. 154

Surrender at Yorktown by John Trumbull (painting detail)
American; 1787; Original at the Detroit Institute of Arts.
This watercolor sketch is the earliest showing a stars and stripes flag of at least five versions of this scene painted by Trumbull. See numbers 32 and 42, below. The Detroit Institute of Arts also has another watercolor sketch of this scene by Trumbull with a very undefined US Flag.
Stars: 13 W stars on a B canton arranged in an oval. The painting is too indistinct to determine the number of points on each star.
Canton: extends to the 6th stripe. "Rests" on a R stripe.
Stripes: 13 R-W-B, 5 R, 4 W, and 4 B.
Image source: Silverman, pg. 46

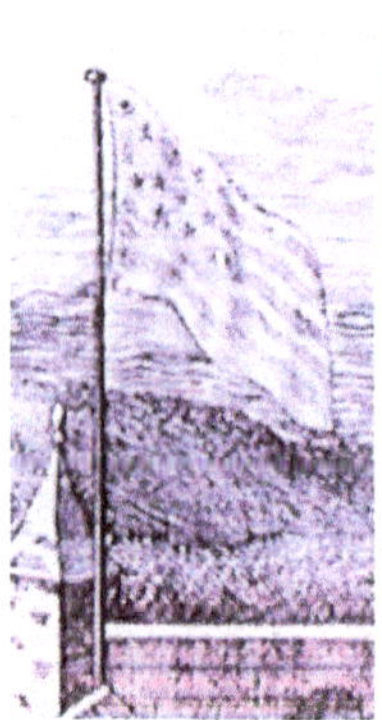

1. American Colours in *Heraldry* by William Fox (manuscript)
British; 1785; Original in the files of the Flag Research Center.
This watercolor painting includes the heraldic blazon.
Stars: 13 multipointed (probably intended to be 8-pointed) described as W, arranged in rows of 3-2-3-2-3 (staggered).
Canton: B, extends to the 4th stripe. "Rests" on a R stripe.
Stripes: 13 described as R-W, 7 R and 6 W.
Image source: FB, pg. 57.
Note: This image was added subsequent to the original article, hence the numerical designation 23.1.

2. Engraved frontispiece of *Proceedings of the Pennsylvania Society of the Cincinnati* engraved by Robert Scot, published by John Steele, Philadelphia
American; 1785; Original sold at the Swann Auction Galleries, Feb 2nd, 2006 for $1,400.
This engraving includes the National Society of the Cincinnati Arms.
Stars: 13 multipointed (probably intended to be 6-pointed) W, arranged in rows of 3-2-3-2-3 (staggered).
Canton: Probably B, extends to the 5th stripe. "Rests" on a W stripe.
Stripes: 13 probably R-W, 7 dark and 6 W.
Image source: Swann Galleries, Inc.
Note: This image was added subsequent to the original article, hence the numerical designation 23.2.

26 and 32, above. The fourth is the very large painting in the US Capitol painted between 1817 and 1824 (closely--but not exactly--modeled after this painting).

Stars: 13 W eight-pointed stars on a B canton arranged with 12 in a square and one in the center.

Canton: apparently extends to the 6th stripe. "Rests" on a R stripe.

Stripes: the stripes on the flag in this painting were painted in such a way as to be of various numbers depending on which part of the flag you are examining. In one place, there appears to be 14 stripes; in another there appears to be 18. They alternate R-W and there appears to be an even number of each.

Image source: Silverman, pg. 47

Battle of Cowpens by Frederick Kemmelmeyer (painting detail)
American; 1795-1800? Original at Yale University.

It should be noted that this painting also depicts an incorrect British Union Flag. Generally, it is believed Kemmelmeyer painted his works before 1800, but the 17 stripes on this flag suggests possibly later, between 1803 and 1812. See # 22.

Stars: apparently 13 W stars on a B canton arranged either in a square or a circle with one in the center. Scale is too small to determine exact number or the number of points on each star.

Canton: extends to the 7th stripe. "Rests" on a W stripe.

Stripes: 17 R-W, 9 R and 8 W.

Image source: Aikman, pg. 97

IMAGE SOURCES

Aikman:
    NEW STARS FOR OLD GLORY by Lonnelle Aikman [National Geographic Society Magazine, Washington DC; July 1959; Vol CXVI No 1]

Cooper:
    THIRTEEN STAR FLAGS - KEYS TO IDENTIFICATION by Grace Rogers Cooper [Smithsonian Institution Press, Washington DC; 1973; First Edition]

FB:
    THE FLAG BULLETIN XII:2, Summer 1973 [Flag Research Center, Winchester MA 01890] - Image from a hand drawn manuscript in the FRC files

Furlong:
    SO PROUDLY WE HAIL - THE HISTORY OF THE UNITED STATES FLAG by William Furlong and Byron McCandless, edited by Harold Langley [Smithsonian Institute Press, Washington DC; 1981; First Edition; ISBN 0-87474-448-2]

Leeper:
    AMERICAN PROCESSIONAL: HISTORY ON CANVAS by John and Blanche Leeper [National Geographic Society Magazine, Washington DC; Feb 1951; Vol XCIX No 2]

Mastai:
    THE STARS AND THE STRIPES by Boleslaw and Marie-Louise D'Otrange Mastai [Alfred A. Knopf, New York NY; 1973; First Edition; ISBN 0-394-472179]

McDowell:
    THE REVOLUTIONARY WAR by Bart McDowell [National Geographic Society, Washington DC; 1967; First Edition]

NAVA:
    NAVA NEWS [North American Vexillological Association, Trenton, NJ, published continuously since 1967, ISSN 1053-3338]

Quaife:
    THE HISTORY OF THE UNITED STATES FLAG by Milo M. Quaife, Melvin J. Weig, Roy E. Appleman [Harper & Row, New York NY; 1961; First Edition]

Richardson:
    STANDARDS AND COLORS OF THE AMERICAN REVOLUTION by Edward W. Richardson [U of PA Press & PA Sons of Revolution, Philadelphia PA; 1982; First Edition; ISBN 0-8122-7839-9]

Diploma for Society of Cincinnati (engraving detail)
French; 1785?; Original owned by the Society of the Cincinnati.
The original is a monochrome engraving. It is possible that this flag was not intended to be that of the US, but rather that of the Society which is of the same design illustrated with blue and white stripes. It was adopted in 1786 but may have been in the design stage earlier.
Stars: 13 five-pointed dark stars on a light canton arranged in two arcs of 8 over 5 above the US Eagle Coat of Arms.
Canton: extends to the 5th stripe. "Rests" on a dark stripe.
Stripes: 13 alternate light and dark, 7 light and 6 dark.
Image source: Richardson, pg. 36

1. U.S. Ensigns (and pennant and jack) in engraving made at Philadelphia.
American; dated 1785.
This engraving is part of a nautical scene.

Tavola delle piu esatte, edusitate Bandiere ... Vinco. Scotti di Livonno l'Anno 1796 (detail)
Italian; 1796; Original at Brown University.
Known as the Scotti Flag Sheet. The five flag illustrations are hand colored.
Stars: 12 W four-pointed stars on a B canton and a R cross of St. George (fimbriated W) bearing a 13th star in the center. The stars are arranged diagonally in imitation of the Cross of St. Andrew.
Canton: extends half way into the 7th stripe. "Rests" half way into a R stripe.
Stripes: 13 R-W, 7 R and 6 W.
Image source: Smith, pgs. 192-193

Tavola delle piu esatte, edusitate Bandiere ... Vinco. Scotti di Livonno l'Anno 1796 (detail)
Italian; 1796; Original at Brown University.
Known as the Scotti Flag Sheet. The five flag illustrations are hand colored.
Stars: 13 W four-pointed stars on a B vertical stripe at the hoist, arranged in 2 vertical rows of 7-6 (staggered).
Canton: none.
Stripes: 13 R-W, 7 R and 6 W.
Image source: Smith, pgs. 192-193

Surrender at Yorktown by John Trumbull (painting detail)
American; 1797; Original at Yale University.
This painting is the third showing a stars and stripes flag of at least five versions of this scene painted by Trumt

New and Correct Map of the United States of North America by Abel Buell (cartouche detail)
American; 1784; Original in the New Jersey Historical Society. The flag illustration is hand colored.
Stars: 13 five-pointed W mullets (stars with a circle piercing the center) on a B canton arranged 3-2-3-2-3 (staggered).
Canton: extends to the 7th stripe. "Rests" on a W stripe.
Stripes: 13 R-W, 7 R and 6 W.
Image source: Mastai, pg. 48

General Schuyler's Flag (canton detail)
American; 1784; Original at Independence National Historical Park.
Flag has a heavy red fringe around three sides. Although consistently dated by experts to the period "after 1784," it should be noted the shield on the US Arms bears 17 pales, the correct number for the period 1803-1812. It is this author's opinion that this flag dates from this later period.
Stars: 13 W stars, twelve five-pointed and one six-pointed (the last one) arranged in an arc over the Eagle.
Canton: extends to the 6th stripe. "Rests" on a W stripe.
Stripes: 13 W-R, 7 W and 6 R.
Image source: Richardson, pg. 189

Tavola delle piu esatte, edusitate Bandiere ... Vinco. Scotti di Livonno l'Anno 1796 (detail)
Italian; 1796; Original at Brown University.
Known as the Scotti Flag Sheet. The five flag illustrations are hand colored.
Also included in this illustration is an American pennant.
Stars: 13 W four-pointed stars on a B canton arranged 4-5-4 such that 4 stars in each row are centered over each other and the 13th star is placed in the center of the fly end of the canton.
Canton: extends to the 7th stripe. "Rests" on a W stripe.
Stripes: 13 R-W, 7 R and 6 W.
Image source: Smith, pgs. 192-193

Tavola delle piu esatte, edusitate Bandiere ... Vinco. Scotti di Livonno l'Anno 1796 (detail)
Italian; 1796; Original at Brown University.
Known as the Scotti Flag Sheet. The five flag illustrations are hand colored.
Stars: 13 W four-pointed stars on a B canton arranged in vertical rows of 4-2-1-2-4 (staggered vertically).
Canton: extends to the 6th stripe. "Rests" on a R stripe.
Stripes: 13 R-B-W, 5 R, 4 W and 4 B.
Image source: Smith, pgs. 192-193

Tavola delle piu esatte, edusitate Bandiere ... Vinco. Scotti di Livonno l'Anno 1796 (detail)
Stars: 13 W four-pointed stars on alternate squares of W and B (7 W and 6 B) at the hoist.
Canton: none.
Stripes: 13 R-W, 7 R and 6 W.
Image source: Smith, pgs. 192-193

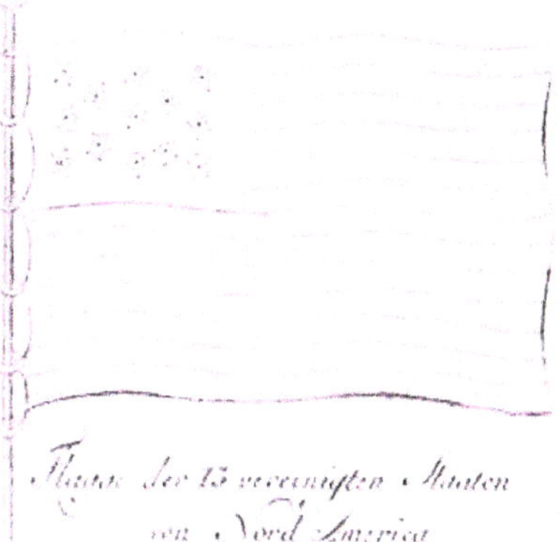

. Historic Geneological Calendar, or Year Book of the Most Curious New Events in the World for 1784 (detail)
German; 1784; Original at Brown University.
Published by Haude and Spener at Berlin, this book contains twelve copper plate engravings of incidents of the American Revolution illustrating an account written by Matthias Sprengel, a professor at the University of Halle. The flag illustration is hand colored in some editions.
Stars: 13 five-pointed W mullets (see #21, above) on a B canton arranged 3-2-3-2-3 (staggered).
Canton: extends to the 6th stripe. "Rests" on a R stripe.
Stripes: 13 R-B-W, 5 R, 4 B and 4 W.
Image source: Color image: Richardson, pg. 198; Black & White image: Matthew Larson

Washington, Lafayette and Tilgman at Yorktown by Charles Wilson Peale (painting detail)
American; 1784; Original at the Maryland State House.
Peale also painted a portrait of Washington at Trenton in the same period showing a similar flag and a portrait of Samuel Smith showing what appears to be the Society of the Cincinnati flag, which is similar in design but has blue and white stripes and a white canton.
Stars: owing to a small scale, it is hard to determine but appears to depict 13 W stars on a B canton arranged above the US Arms.
Canton: extends to the 5th stripe. "Rests" on a W stripe.
Stripes: 13 R-W, 7 R and 6 W.
Image source: Richardson, pg. 188

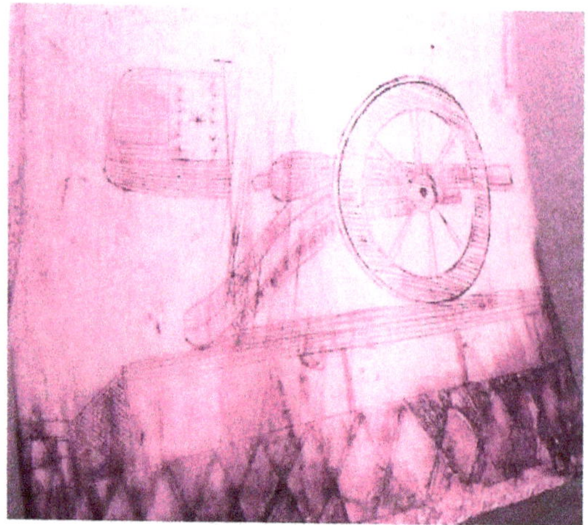

1. Flag on David Shaw's Powder Horn (engraving detail)
American; 1779 Nov. 28; Original sold in the Americana Auction by Cowan's Auctions Inc.,
December 2, 2004, Cincinnati, Ohio for $3,500.
The flag is engraved as black lines on the horn.
Stars: 13, 12 depicted as 6-pointed and the center star depicted as 8-pointed, arranged in two vertical rows of 6 stars with one
placed centered between the rows. The stars are engraved and colored black.
Canton: Extends about two-thirds of the way down the flag. Hard to tell how many stripes down.
Stripes: Appears to be more than 30, although some of the lines may be intended to indicate the flag is waving and not stripes.
Exact number of stripes is not clear.
Image source: Cowan's Auctions, Inc.
Note: This image was added subsequent to the original article, hence the numerical designation 4.1.

Harmon Stebens Powder Horn (engraving detail)
American; 1779; Original at the Smithsonian Institution.
Original is a monochrome engraving. Design consists of a grouping of four US Flags.
Stars: all are dark stars on a light canton, the first has 13 arranged 4-4-5 (even), the second has 13 arranged 4-4-3-2 (staggered), the
third has 12 arranged 4-3-5 (staggered) and the fourth has 14 arranged 5-4-3-2 (upper two rows even and lower two rows
staggered). Number of points indeterminate.
Canton: the two flags that show completely have the canton extended to the 6th stripe. "Rests" on a dark stripe.
Stripes: The first and fourth flags are shown in their entirety and both have 13 stripes, alternate dark and light, 7 dark and 6 light.
The second and third flags are shown "cut off" such that you cannot see any stripes past the end of the cantons. They show 7 stripes
each below the canton, alternate dark and light, 4 dark and 3 light.
Image source: Furlong, pg. 129

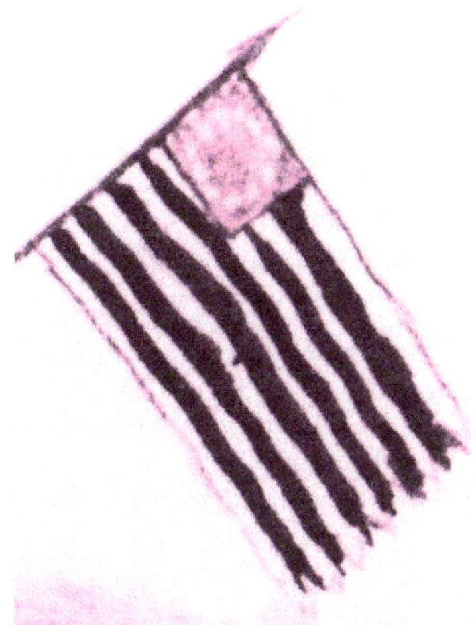

Barton's Second Seal Design (painting detail)
American; 1782; Original at United States National Archives.
William Barton's first design no longer exists but it also included a flag with a circle of stars. Regarding the first design he wrote that the stars represent "a new Constellation. ... Their Disposition, in the form of a Circle, denotes the Perpetuity of its Continuance, the Ring being the Symbol of Eternity."
Stars: 13 W stars on B canton arranged in circle. The stars are too small to determine the number of points but the border of the shield on the seal contains 13 eight pointed stars.
Canton: extends to the center of the 5th stripe. Doesn't "Rest" on any stripe.
Stripes: 13 alternate W-R, 7 W and 6 R.
Image source: Furlong, pg. 139

Map of Yorktown by Maj. Sebastian Bauman (cartouche detail)
American; 1782; Original at Brown University. The flag illustration is hand colored.
Stars: 13 W stars on B canton, arranged 3-2-3-2-3 (staggered). They appear to be eight-pointed but the scale is very small.
Canton: extends to the 4th stripe. "Rests" on a W stripe.
Stripes: 11 stripes are visible alternate W-R, 6 W and 5 R.
Image source: Mastai, pg. 45

Abraham Weatherwise's Town and Country Almanack (engraving detail)
American; 1782; Original at the Library of Congress.
Abraham Weatherwise was the pseudonym of David Rittenhouse and the Almanack was published at Boston. The original is a monochrome engraving.
Stars: 13 five-pointed dark stars on a light canton arranged 3-5-5 (even with top row over the last three stars of the other two rows).

Canton: extends to the 8th stripe. "Rests" on a light stripe.
Stripes: 29 alternate light-dark, 15 light and 14 dark. Widths of stripes varies somewhat.
Image source: Furlong, pg. 138

Map of the United States by John Wallis (cartouche detail)
British; 1783 Apr. 3; Original at Henry F. DuPont Winterthur Museum.
The original is a monochrome engraved print. The flag illustration is hand colored.
Stars: 13 four-pointed stars, W on B, arranged 3-2-3-2-3 (staggered).
Canton: extends to the center of the 7th stripe. "Rests" in the center of a W stripe.
Stripes: 13 W-R, 7 W and 6 R.
Image source: Furlong, pg. 150

Stripes: 13 alternate R-W, 7 R and 6 W.
Image source: Mastai, pg. 48

Tableau de tous les Pavillons que lon arbore sur les Vaisseaux dans Quatre Parties du Monde É (detail)
French; 1781; Original at Brown University.
Also known as the Mondhare Flag Sheet. The flag illustration is hand colored.
Stars: 12 probably five-pointed (the artist was very sloppy and simply painted a "box" around each star) W stars on a B canton,
arranged 3-3-3-3 (even) plus one gold Fleur-di-lis at the center top of the canton.
Canton: extends to the 11th stripe. "Rests" on a W stripe.
Stripes: 13 alternate R-W, 7 R and 6 W.
Image source: Quaife, pg. 55

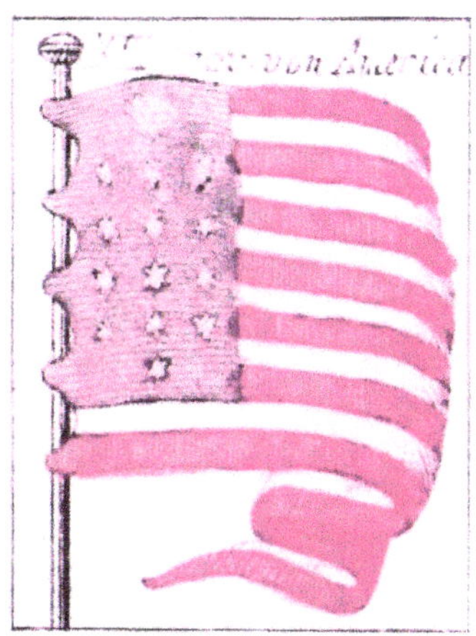

Flaggen aller Seefhrenden Potensen und Nationen in der gantzen Welt (detail)
German; 1782; Original at Brown University.
Also known as the Lotter Flag Sheet. The flag illustration is hand colored.
Stars: 13 six-pointed W stars on a B canton arranged 3-3-3-3-1 (even with last star centered) plus one gold Fleur-di-lis at the center
top of the canton.
Canton: extends to the 11th stripe. "Rests" on a W stripe.
Stripes: 13 alternate R-W, 7 R and 6 W.
Image source: Mastai, pg. 36

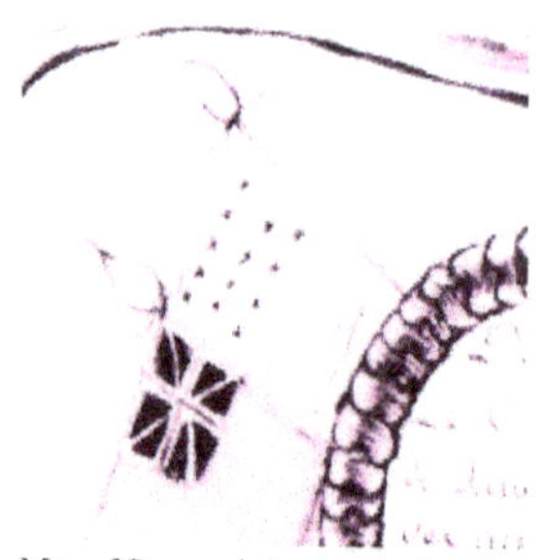

Map of Savannah (cartouche detail)
French; 1780 June 15; Original at the Newberry Library.
Original depicts the US Flag in a line drawing.
Stars: 13 dark on light, apparently some having six and some eight points, arranged 5-4-4 (staggered).
Canton: the flag is shown "cut off" such that you cannot see any stripes past the fly end of the canton. Assuming 13 stripes, the canton extends to the 6th stripe.
Stripes: below the canton there appears to be eight stripes.
Image source: Furlong, pg. 132

View of the American Position at Yorktown by Lt. John Graves Simcoe (painting detail)
British; 1781? Original at Colonial Williamsburg.
It should be noted that this small painting, painted by a British soldier across the river from the American lines, also depicts two incorrect British Union Flags, one upside-down Dutch flag and one correct British White Ensign.
Stars: Indistinct dark stars on a blue canton.
Canton: extends to the 10th stripe. "Rests" on a R stripe.
Stripes: 13, alternate R-B, 7 R and 6 B.
Image source: Aikman, pg. 100

Fort Independence Flag (also known as the Jonathan Fowle Flag)
American; 1781; Original at the Massachusetts State House.
This is the flag used in 1791 to receive the first British salute from a Man-of-War to the US flag.
Stars: 13 five-pointed W stars on a B canton, arranged 4-5-4 (even).
Canton: extends to the 7th stripe. "Rests" on a W stripe.

Regimental colors and the so-called Valley Forge Flag of Washington's Headquarters. The former two cannot be dated with certainty any earlier than 1784 and the latter is suspected by some experts to be the canton from a possibly later Stars and Stripes. Primarily the stars in Revolutionary War America were arranged in three rows, usually 4-5-4. After the War, this arrangement still predominated but the circle or oval of stars was nearly as popular. Only two show 3-2-3-2-3. Stripe colors in the American sources are exclusively red and white during the War (almost all beginning and ending with red) and nearly so afterwards although there are more beginning and ending with white. Only one American source shows a tricolor stripe arrangement, dating from 1787. It should be noted that the two Dutch paintings of the flags of the "Alliance" and the "Serapis" were believed to have been painted from life with some measure of accuracy and would both be the exceptions to this sense, although it is suspected one or both flags were not made in America.

Considering the number of points on the stars, it is a mixed bag and would appear that any number was used, even different numbers of points on the stars of a single flag (see 4 and 28, below, for example). The size of the cantons is also very variable, with no clear preference. It is interesting to note that there are three flags with red and blue stripes, all associated with southern states (numbers 7, 33 and 34, below). After the Revolutionary War, the star arrangements are very mixed. Indeed, even different illustrations by the same person vary greatly (see 26, 27, 32 and 42, below, for example).

Among the European sources, the flag designs are somewhat different, with stars in rows of 3-2-3-2-3 being exclusive in the British sources and nearly so in the German sources. The German sources mostly show tri-colored stripes as well. The so-called "French Alliance Flag" bearing a gold fleur-de-lys as well as the stars is shown only in two French and one German source in the period 1781-83. No American source shows it.

Addenda: Since the above was written in 2000, eleven additional illustrations have surfaced (included below) that have offered some further information that seems to basically confirm the conclusions above. Of these illustrations, seven are American (numbers 1.1, 4.1, 23.2, 24.1, 26.1, 29.1, and 32.1 below) and only one of them shows the stars in rows of 3-2-3-2-3 (dated 1785). The other four are all British (numbers 23.1, 35.1, 35.2, and 35.3) and they all show this arrangement! Again, the star points are a mixed bag, although the majority of them seem to be five-pointed.

Note: the following conventions are used in this presentation: "even" means the rows of stars begin and end vertically in line with other rows, even if there are different numbers of stars; "staggered" means the stars are set equidistant from each other in each row causing some rows to be shorter and some to be longer horizontally; "R" means red; "W" means white and "B" means blue. See the listing of image source codes.

Chester County PA Militia Color (Battle of Brandywine)
American; 1777 Sept. 11; Original at Independence National Historical Park.
Field of solid red with stars and stripes canton.
Stars: 13 eight-pointed R stars on W canton arranged 4-5-4 (even). Two upperhoistmost stars appear cut off.
Canton: extends to 5th stripe. "Rests" on a W stripe.
Stripes: 13 W-R. 7 W and 6 R.
Image source: Furlong, pg. 114

Flag of the "Alliance" at The Texel Holland (painting)
Dutch; 1779 Oct. 4; Original at the Chicago Historical Society.
Stars: 13 eight-pointed W stars on B canton arranged 3-2-3-2-3 (staggered).
Canton: extends to 6th stripe. "Rests" on a W stripe.
Stripes: 13 W-R, 7 W and 6 R.
Image source: Sedeen, pg. 47

Flag of the "Serapis" at The Texel Holland (painting)
Dutch; 1779 Oct. 5; Original at the Chicago Historical Society.
Stars: 13, 12 eight-pointed and 1 seven-pointed (second star in top row) W stars on B canton arranged 4-5-4 (staggered).
Canton: extends to 5th stripe. "Rests" on a B stripe.
Stripes: 13 irregularly colored B-R-W-R-W-B-R-W-R-B-W-B-R, making 4 B, 5 R and 4 W.
Image source: Sedeen, pg. 47

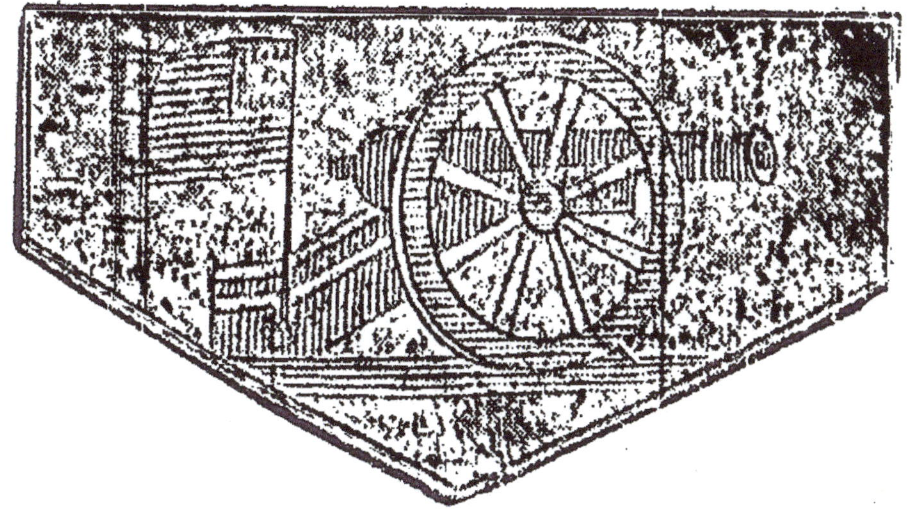

1. Brass Artillery Cap Plate
American; 1779; Two original plates excavated at the Pluckemin archeological dig in Bedminister, New Jersey in 1979.
The flag is engraved as a line drawing on the plates.
The dig was reported in the local newspapers and that is the original source for the illustration. The site was occupied by the American artillery from December 7, 1778 until early June 1777. These items were found among other items of brass waste and it is concluded they were made on site.
Stars: 13 arranged in even rows of 5-3-5, with the center row of stars centered under the first, third, and fifth stars in the other rows. No colors are indicated. Details too small to make out number of points.
Canton: Extends to the 7th stripe.
Stripes: Twelve, no colors indicated. There are 7 stripes next to the canton and 5 below it.
Image source: NAVA NEWS, Volume XXI, No. 4 (Number 98), July/August 1988, pg. 1
Note: This image was added subsequent to the original article, hence the numerical designation 1.1.

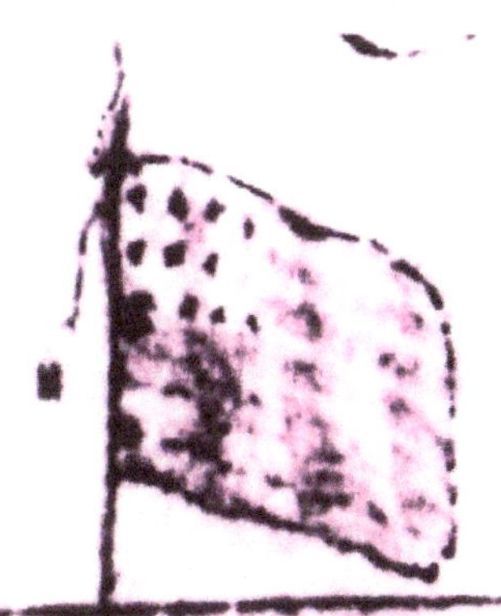

Order of Battle, Maj. Gen. Sullivan's Army by Maj. John Ross (sketch detail)
American; 1779 July 30; Original at the Pennsylvania Historical Society.
Original is a monochrome sketch.
Stars: 12 dark stars on a light canton arranged 4-4-4 (even). Details too small to make out number of points.
Canton: extends to 6th stripe. "Rests" on a dark stripe.
Stripes: 13 alternate dark-light, 7 dark and 6 light.
Image source: Richardson, pg. 27

A Proclamation of Independence

We, therefore, the representatives of the United States of America, in General Congress, assembled, appealing to the Supreme Judge of the world for the rectitude of our intentions, do, in the name, and by the authority of the good people of these colonies, solemnly publish and declare, that these united colonies are, and of right ought to be free and independent states; that they are absolved from all allegiance to the British Crown, and that all political connection between them and the state of Great Britain, is and ought to be totally dissolved; and that as free and independent states, they have full power to levy war, conclude peace, contract alliances, establish commerce, and to do all other acts and things which independent states may of right do. And for the support of this declaration, with a firm reliance on the protection of Divine Providence, we mutually pledge to each other our lives, our fortunes, and our sacred honor.

Signed by John Hancock of Massachusetts, President of the Congress, and by the fifty-five other Representatives of the thirteen United States of America.

Good Morning,

    I can vividly recall, as a child, viewing a parade in my
hometown. The crowd stood by the curb anxiously waiting as the
sound of music came ever closer. Finally, I felt my heart jump, my
body chill. Some of the people saluted, while others placed a hand
on their heart. It was the Flag!

    To this day, whether it's a parade, a concert, or a ballgame, I
thrill to the sight of our Flag. And I have a feeling that you feel
the same way that I do.

    I see more than Stars and Stripes. I see lakes and hills. I
see a cousin who died in Vietnam. I see country fairs and shopping
malls. Most of all I see a home where my children can play, laugh
and live without fear.

    There was a time not long ago when people would laugh at this
kind of old-fashioned patriotism. Some people even trampled and
burned flags. But no more!

    Today we see a new birth of patriotic fervor, and crowds openly
and enthusiastically cheering the Flag. Yes, Americans cheer their
Flag - and what it stands for: Freedom. Plenty. Pride.

    It's needed. It's something that <u>you</u> can do for your country.

    Please help.